PUFFIN BOOKS

Editor: Kaye Webb

THE DEVIL'S CHILDREN

Nicky Gore had been alone in London for almost a
month. The last person to whom she'd talked was
an old man who was dying. He told her not to go
past his house after his death or she might catch
the same disease. So round and round she swung on
one heel in the park. Round and round and round.
Suddenly she heard voices. She didn't understand
the language, but before long she discovered they
could speak hers (although they didn't seem very
friendly). She ran back to her house and pinned a
message for her parents on the door. 'I'm going
away now. I waited for twenty-eight days.'

This is a book about the time when everyone in
England turned violently against any sort of modern
machinery, and cars, buses and trains disappeared
from life because they were regarded as evil.

Nicky and the Devil's Children, wandering no-
mads who become the only family she has, have
to deal with all sorts of problems and there are
many kinds of dramatic collisions along the way.

The Devil's Children

PETER DICKINSON

Illustrated by Robert Hales

PUFFIN BOOKS

Puffin Books: a Division of Penguin Books Ltd,
Harmondsworth, Middlesex, England
Penguin Books Australia Ltd, Ringwood, Victoria, Australia
Penguin Books Canada Ltd, 41 Steelcase Road West, Markham, Ontario, Canada
Penguin Books (N.Z.) Ltd, 182-190 Wairau Road, Auckland 10, New Zealand

—

First published by Victor Gollancz 1970
Published in Puffin Books 1972
Reprinted 1974

—

Copyright © Peter Dickinson, 1970
Illustrations © Robert Hales, 1970

—

Made and printed in Great Britain by
Hazell Watson & Viney Ltd
Aylesbury, Bucks
Set in Linotype Pilgrim

for
RANI GAGAN DEEP SINGH

CONTENTS

INTRODUCTION

THIS is the third book I have written about the Changes — the time when the English turn furiously against every sort of machine. If you want to know why they did so, and how the Changes ended, you will have to read *The Weather-monger*. If you want to know what England was like when we'd all got used to living without machines, you can read *Heartsease*. But this book is about the very beginning of the Changes, while this island was still settling down to its new pattern.

There is a real village exactly like Felpham. The church has a brick tower, and stands among limes with a school beside it; there is a large white house at one end of the village, and at the other end a lane curls up a long slope, runs below a double row of pylons and comes to a farm. My brother and I built the well-head on page 58 with our own hands. I have altered very little.

But I've had to change the name of the village, and all the other names around. I don't want anyone to think that the people I've put in this story are the people who really live in the village which isn't called Felpham. Even in terrible times like the ones I've described, I'm sure that my friends who live there would be both braver and kinder.

7 May 1969   PETER DICKINSON

1

BECOMING A CANARY

'NICOLA GORE,' said Nicky. 'I am Nicola Gore.'

She turned on her right heel, kicking herself round and round with her left foot, until the leather of the heel began to drill a neat, satisfying hole among the roots of the six-inch grass.

'Nicola Gore,' she said as she spun. 'Nicola Gore. Nicola Gore. Nicola Gore.'

She was talking to herself, of course, because there was no one else to talk to. The last living person she'd seen had been the one-legged old man who sat on his doorstep in the sun, waiting to die and talking about his boyhood in Hammersmith sixty years ago, when the noise of London traffic had been the rattle and grate of iron wheels on cobbles.

Now the only noise was birdsong, and Nicky saying her own name to herself, aloud in the enormous loneliness.

The old man had gone from his doorstep twelve days ago. She had promised not to try and look for him, because he had said his going would be the sign.

And it was nineteen days before that since she'd last talked to anyone she really knew, anyone who loved her. She turned and turned. It was taking longer to get dizzy now than it had when she'd first discovered the trick.

They weren't going to come and find her now, were they? She'd done what she'd always been told to, if ever she was lost — waited where she'd last seen Mummy and Daddy, waited for a day and a night and another day, watching the dull-eyed ranks of refugees straggle towards Dover. Then she had set her chin and walked the other way, back to the drained city, looking at all the faces of the people who were leaving but not answering any questions, no matter how kindly. If she went *home*, someone would come and look for her, surely.

But they hadn't.

Just in time, before the tears came, the long wave of dizziness began to wash over her. Nicky had discovered this trick quite early. If you could get yourself dizzy enough, you stopped being Nicola Gore, alone and frightened and miserable in great empty London, and you became a sort of daze without a name, a blurred bit of a blurred world. She went on turning as long as she could still stand.

When the blurs began to settle into shapes again they were the tops of trees. She lay on her back in the spider-peopled grass and looked at the blue, unmottled sky. It had been like that every day, except for the hideous thunder-storm on the road to Dover. Would it last for ever? No, it was July now, but one day it would be winter. She'd have to go before then. She ought to go now, before she caught the sickness down the road, or another sickness from living on lemonade and crisps and nuts looted out of empty pubs. She must set her chin again, become hard and uncaring, endure a world of strangers.

She knew that when it came to leaving she would need something to *make* her, but the impulse to action levered her out of the grass. Listlessly she looked round the place which five weeks ago had been called Shepherd's Bush Green, London, W.14. A four-acre triangle of turf, criss-crossed with paths and dotted with trees; round it ran a wide road; blank shops lined the northern side, and unfin-ished towers of flats and offices rose to the south. Nasty engines squatted in the road, silent and useless; they were all dead, since the people who had once made them work and move had left, but even so Nicky preferred not to go near them. Luckily there were gaps between them, where Nicky could tip-toe through, then scamper along the pavement of Shepherd's Bush Road, round the corner and home.

That's where she ought to be now, waiting in case they came after all, but it was better here among the trees. This was where you could get furthest from the dead machines and the black unnatural roads that stank strangely under the downright sun. And she *had* pinned her notice to the door, saying where she was, just as she'd done for the last twenty-eight days. Still, perhaps she'd better go and see.

She turned listlessly on her heel, knowing it was useless and that she would have to make the effort not to cry when she got there and found the notice untouched. Dully she kept turning, like a slow top, and felt her heel beginning to bite yet another neat round hole into the earth below the squashed grass.

About the ninth time she went round she saw a movement up at the east end of the Green.

At first she thought that it was just the dizziness, coming sooner than usual and making the world tilt about, but next time round she stopped being a top and stood swaying and peering. The movement was people.

For no reason she slid towards the nearest tree-trunk and hid.

There were quite a lot of them, and the colours were wrong. It was like a procession in fancy dress. All the men had beards, and they wore mauve and pink and purple hats. No, not hats. There was a word for them . . . And there was a word for the women's bright, slim dresses, which reached right down to their ankles . . . and another word for these people, with their strange clothes and beards and brown skins ... or was it all something she had once dreamed she knew about? There were blank bits in her mind nowadays. Perhaps it was the loneliness.

Four of the men came in front, carrying heavy sticks; behind them marched a big group pushing carts and prams or carrying bright-coloured bundles, several children walked among the prams; one cart was covered with cushions, on which an old lady was propped up; at the back came another four men, also armed with heavy sticks. They moved very slowly, like a funeral, along the north side of the Green. They were quite silent, apart from the iron wheels of the hand-carts grating on the tarmac, until they were nearly opposite where Nicky was hiding. Then a high voice shrieked an incomprehensible sentence from amid the group of prams and the whole procession halted. They all began talking together as they spread themselves out on the grass, sat down and started to eat the food which the women passed among them.

They looked very strange, very different from anyone Nicky had ever known.

But they were people, and they were going somewhere.

Her mind made itself up without being asked. She slipped away along the tree-trunks, over the road to her gap between the bad machines, along the pavement to where the old traffic lights stood blind as stone, left down Shepherd's Bush Road — walking now, and panting with the heat, and her neck sore from where the collar of her filthy shirt stuck to the sweaty skin — and along her home street.

Not home any more. The street was dead, and buzzing with flies in the stinking, tarry heat.

Yes, her note was pinned to the pink door, untouched; but this time she didn't feel her throat narrowing and her eyes peppery with useless tears. She pushed the door open and ran up the stairs to her own room. Even this, with its brown carpet and the pictures of ships on the walls, didn't feel like home now. She took her satchel from the shelf, wiped the dust off it with her sleeve, undid the straps and tilted the meaningless books out on to the floor. Into the bottom of the satchel she stuffed a jersey, a spare skirt, her party blouse, the socks she's managed to wash in soda-water, and her gym shoes.

Anything else which she needed or wanted? Not Teddy, comfort though he'd been. None of the school uniform. Nothing to make her remember home or Mummy or Daddy. That was all over now – it had happened to some-body else, a girl with parents to love her and look after her. But Nicola Gore was going to look after herself, and not let anybody love her again, ever. It wasn't worth the loss.

Out of her desk drawer she took the blunt hunting knife which she'd bought with her own money at the fair when she was staying with Granny at Hertford; and from the blue jar on the mantelpiece she took the coral-and-gold necklace which one of her godmothers had given her at her christen-ing, but she could never remember which.

Then she ran down to the kitchen, picking her way to the larder between the horrible smashed machines. Two bottles of lemonade and one of soda-water from her last pub raid; the packets of nuts and the salty biscuits. Her satchel was full now, and heavy too. She slung its strap over her shoul-der, picked up her pencil from the hall table and pushed the door wide open until she could lean against it to write on her notice without it moving away.

She crossed out her last message, about being up at the Green, and wrote beneath it, 'I'm going away now. I waited for twenty-eight days.'

She was pulling the door shut when she thought that that

sounded as though she was blaming them, so she pushed it open again and wrote underneath 'I'm sure you would have come if you could. Love Nicky.'

When she pulled the door shut for the last time she felt that there ought to be some way of fastening it, but she couldn't remember how the lock worked. So she just made certain that the drawing-pins were firmly fastened into her note, turned away and walked down the street without once looking back. She started to be afraid that she would be too late, but it was awkward to run with her satchel so heavy. It didn't matter; they were still there when she reached the Green again; the strange, dark children were playing a game of 'touch' under the trees.

Beyond them the adults lolled or squatted on the grass. The whole group were chattering like roosting starlings. The noise of their talk bounced off the shop-fronts, and all of a sudden made the Green feel as though people were living there once again.

Yes, thought Nicky, these foreign-looking folk would do. She could go with them, and yet stay strangers always. It was a good thing they were so different. She sidled like a hunter towards the scampering children.

She was waiting by a tree-trunk, beyond the fringe of the game, when one of the smaller boys scuttered from an exploding group which the 'he' had raided. He came straight towards her squealing with laughter until he was hardly six feet away; and then he saw her. At once he stopped dead, called with a shrill new note, and pointed at her. Then he stood staring. His eyes were very dark; his hair was black and gathered into a little top-knot behind his head. His skin looked smooth as silk and was a curious, pale brown – not the yellow-brown of suntan, but a greyer colour, as if it was always like that. His mouth pouted.

The game stopped at his call, not quite at once, but in spasms of scuttering which stilled into the same dark stare. Now the adults' heads were turning too; the thick beards wagging round; the worried, triangular faces of the women turning towards Nicky. One of the women called: two children ran to her side and stared from there. The other children melted back towards the adults, looking over their shoulders once or twice. Several of the men were on their feet, grasping their heavy staves and peering not at her but up and down the Green. Now the whole group were standing, except for the little old woman who had ridden on the cart; she still sat on the ground and gazed with piercing fierceness at Nicky from among the legs of the men. Then she cried out suddenly, only three or four words, like the call of a bird. The words were not English.

A big man bent and scooped her off the grass, like a mother picking up her baby; he carried her to the cushioned cart, which was brightly painted with swirling patterns – it was the sort of hand-cart that street-market stall-holders had used for pushing their goods about. The old woman settled herself on the cushions, stared at Nicky again, and called another few words. At once the whole group trooped off the grass and took up their positions for the march.

Nicky ran forward from under the trees. They were all watching her still, as though she might be the bait in some unimaginable trap.

'Please,' she called. 'May I come with you?'

A rustle ran through the group like the rustle of dead leaves stirring under a finger of wind. One of the worried women said something, and three of the men answered her. Nicky could tell from their voices that they were disagreeing with her. The old woman spoke a single syllable, and the nearest man shook his head at Nicky. He was short and fat and his beard was flecked with grey; his hat was pink, only it wasn't a hat, of course – it was a long piece of cloth wound in and out of itself in clever folds to cover his head and hair.

'Please,' she said again. 'I'm all alone and I don't know where to go.'

'Go away, little girl,' said the fat man. 'We cannot help you. You are not one of us. We owe you nothing.'

His voice was light and odd. Though he spoke proper English, he didn't speak it like an Englishman.

'Please,' began Nicky, but the old woman called again and at once the whole group began to move.

They walked off quite slowly, not because they wanted to move like a funeral, but because they couldn't go faster than the slowest child. Nicky stood and watched them, all shrivelled with despair at the thought of facing the huge loneliness of London once again.

She stepped into the road to watch the strange people turn the corner north. (If they'd wanted to go south they would have started down the other side of the Green.) But instead they went straight ahead, up the Uxbridge Road, towards the doorstep where the one-legged man had sat in the sun.

Nicky began to run.

Her sachel dragged her sideways and thudded unsteadily into her hip. A rat-tail of dirty fair hair twisted into her mouth and she spat it out. Her soles slapped on the hot pavement and the echo slapped back at her off the empty shops. When she crossed the big road at the end of the Green the strange people were only a hundred yards down it, so slow was their march. She ran on, gasping.

They must have heard her coming, because one of the four men who walked in the rear came striding towards her, his stave grasped in both hands like a weapon.

'Go away, little girl,' he said sharply. 'We do not want you. We cannot help you.'

Nicky stopped. He was taller and younger than the fat man who had spoken to her before, and frowned at her very fiercely.

'No! Don't go that way!' she said between gasps. 'There's a bad sickness that way. An old man told me. He said he was going to catch the sickness and die. He made me promise not to go down there. He said he'd seen people staggering about and then falling down dead in the street.'

The dark man moved his stave, so that it stopped being a weapon and became a stick to lean on.

'This is true?' he asked.

'Yes, of course.'

He looked at her for several seconds, just as fiercely as before. Then, without another word to her, he turned and called after the procession in the strange language. Beyond him Nicky could see two or three faces turn. A cry came back, the man answered and another cry came. By this time the whole group had stopped.

'Come with me,' said the man without looking round, and strode off up the street. Nicky followed.

Men, women and children stood staring and unsmiling, still as a grove of trees, while she walked between them. When they reached the cushioned cart where the old woman lay the man stopped and spoke for some time. The old woman creaked a few words back at him. Her face was all shrivelled into wrinkles and folds as though it had been soaked too long in water, but her thin hooky nose stood out of the wrinkles like the beak of a hawk, and her dark brown eyes shone with angry life. She looked like a queen witch.

'Tell your story again, please, miss,' said the man.

Nicky had stopped panting, so she could fit her words

together into proper sentences; but she was so afraid of the
old woman that she found she could hardly speak above a
whisper. She felt the other people drawing closer, so as to be
able to hear.

'I used to bring food for an old man who sat on a doorstep,' she said. 'He only had one leg, which is why he hadn't
gone away. He told me that quite a lot of people further
down this road had stayed too, and how they'd got very sick
and if you went near them you might catch their sickness.
It was the sort of sickness you die of, he said. He said that
they crawled out into the street, like rats coming into the
open when they've eaten poison, but some of them danced
and staggered about before they fell down. He made me

promise not to go this way if he wasn't on his doorstep, because that would mean that the sickness had come up the street as far as where he lived. He wasn't here when I came to look for him twelve days ago, and he hasn't come back. That's where he used to sit, down there, opposite the church.'

The group was still no longer, but wavering and rustling. Suddenly the startling clamour of voices broke out, all of them seeming to speak at the same time. The women drew their children close to them, and the men's hands began to gesture in several directions. A younger man with a very glossy beard spoke directly to Nicky, in English.

'Cholera, perhaps,' he said. 'Or plague.'

He sounded interested, as though he'd have liked to explore further up the road and see which guess was right.

The big man who pushed the old woman's cart had pulled a red book from under the cushions and was peering at it amid the clamour; two of the other men, still arguing at the tops of their voices, craned over his shoulders. The old woman held up her arms suddenly and screeched like a wild animal, and the shouting stopped. She asked a short question, and was answered by a mild-faced young woman in a blue dress. The old woman nodded, pointed south, and spoke again. The crowd murmured agreement. The big man ran his finger down a page of the book, flipped over some more pages, and ran his finger on – he must be tracing a road on a map. Then the whole group picked up all they had been carrying; the pram-pushers and cart-pushers circled round; the old woman screeched and they all started back towards the Green. They filed round Nicky as though she were a rock in the road.

She stood, running her thumb back and forward under her satchel strap, and let them trail past. Nobody said a word, and only one or two of the smallest children stared. When the last four, the stave-carriers, had gone she followed behind. One of them glanced over his shoulder and spoke to the man who had led her into the group. He glanced back too, said something, shrugged and walked on. Nicky trudged behind.

They turned right at the Green, south. Their pace was a dreary dawdle as they went down Shepherd's Bush Road, which Nicky had so often scampered along. Carefully she didn't look up the side-street to where her note was pinned to the pink door, but studied instead a gang of scrawny cats which watched from a garden wall on the other side of the road; already they were as wild as squirrels.

Yes, she thought, I am right to go now. If I stay any longer I will become like those cats. She remembered how neat the strange children had seemed, even while they were playing their game of 'touch', and wondered how she herself looked. You can't wash much in soda-water.

At Hammersmith Broadway there had been either an accident or a battle, for two buses lay on their sides and a vegetable lorry had charged into the ruin, scattering crates of lettuce about. The wreckage stank and the procession edged well clear of it. A minute of two later they were on Hammersmith Bridge.

Here the whole group stopped and the adults broke into their cackle of many-voiced argument while the children crowded to the railings and gazed at the still and shining water. Small brown arms pointed at floating gulls or bits of waterlogged driftwood, ignoring the wrangle that raged behind them. Nicky wondered how they could ever decide anything if they were all allowed to speak at the same time. The big man found a sheet of paper under the cushions, a real map with many folds, and this was pored over until, once more, the harsh creak of the old woman decided the question. Mothers called their children to them; burdens were hefted; the march dawdled on.

They went so slowly that Nicky decided she could afford a few minutes more on the bridge, she would be able to catch them without hurrying. The river was beautiful, full from bank to bank as high tide began to ebb unhurriedly towards the sea. A sailing dinghy fidgeted round at its moorings as the water changed direction. Something about the river's calm and shining orderliness washed away all Nicky's resolution – the river ran to the sea, and over the sea lay France, and that's where Mummy and Daddy were, and a little boat like that couldn't be hard to sail. She could swim

out to it and row it ashore, and then stock it up with crisps
and lemonade and sail down the river, round the coast and
over the Channel. And then it would be only a matter of
finding them, among all the millions of strangers. They *must*
have left a message, somewhere. Sailing would be nice –
alone, but going to meet the people who were waiting for
you, who would kiss you and not ask questions and show
you the room they had kept ready for you ...

Nicky's whole skeleton was shaken by a tearing shudder,
like the jerk of nerves that sometimes shocks the body wide
awake just as it is melting into sleep, only this shudder went
on and on. Nicky knew it well. It had shaken her all that first
nightmare morning, and once or twice since. It was a sign
that somewhere a hellish machine was working.

She looked wildly about for a few seconds, not feeling
how her mouth and lips were pulling themselves into a hard
snarl like a dog's, nor how her legs were running down the
street called Castelnau faster than they'd ever run when
she'd asked them, nor how her hand was groping in her
satchel for the hunting-knife.

A bus towered in the road; the strange people crowded
round it, chattering again. Nicky jostled between them and
hurled herself at the young man who stood smiling beside
the vile engine which churned its sick stink and noise into
the air. Her knife was held for killing. The young man was
the only person looking in her direction. He shouted before
she was quite through the crowd, and started to back away
round the bus. A hard thing rammed into her ear and cheek-
bone, jarring her head so that for an instant she could not
see.

In fact she could not remember falling, but now she was
on her hands and knees groping dazedly for the dropped
knife, not finding it, then crawling towards the drumming

engine and feeling again in her satchel for a bottle to hit with.

The world seemed to be shouting. Tough hands gripped her arms and hoisted her up. She struggled towards the bus,

but the hands held her, hard as rope. The young man was climbing again through the door of the bus. She lunged at the hands with her teeth, but the men who held her did so in such a way that she couldn't reach.

All at once the foul drumming stopped, and only the stink of it hung between the houses. A voice croaked an order. They all moved on, up Castelnau.

Slowly, like the panic of nightmare dying as you lie in the half-dark and work out that you really are in your own bed between safe walls, the lust of hatred ebbed. She felt her neck-muscles unlock. Her hands and knees, where she had fallen, stung with sudden pain. She was so tired that she would have dropped, but for the hands that gripped her. She let her head droop.

It might have been a signal for the others to stop, and for the clatter of arguing voices to break out again. Most of the voices were men's, but sometimes a woman joined in. At last something was settled.

'Are you all right now, miss?' said a man.

Nicky nodded.

'Why did you do that?' said the man.

'Do what?'

'Try to kill Kewal?'

'He made the thing go,' she said. 'He mustn't. I had to stop him.'

'Who told you to?'

'I don't know.'

'Do you want to kill him now?'

Nicky looked round the dark, silent faces. The young man she'd charged at stood directly before her, smiling, his small teeth brilliant amid the gorgeous beard. Only one of his eyes looked directly at her. The other one squinted crazily over her right shoulder.

'No,' she said.

'But if he tried to make the bus go again?' asked the man.

'Yes,' she said.

The hands let go of her and she swayed. An arm curled round her shoulders to stop her falling – a woman's arm this time.

'You will come with us,' said the man. It wasn't a question. Now, at last, she looked up and saw the speaker was the big man who had been pushing the old woman on the cart. A woman in a blue dress, the one who'd answered the question about the sickness, knelt down in the road and started to sponge Nicky's bleeding knees.

'Yes,' said the young man, Kewal, smiling and squinting. 'You will be our canary.'

'Kaya?' said one of the women.

'When the miners go into the coalmines,' explained the young man importantly, 'they take a canary with them; if there is firedamp about – that is carbon monoxide, you know – the bird feels it before the miners. Just so this girl ... what is your name, miss?'

'Nicola Gore.'

'Just so Miss Gore will be able to warn us of dangers which we cannot perceive.'

'You are willing?' asked the big man.

'Most people call me Nicky,' she explained.

'Good,' he said, as if she had answered 'Yes'. She had in a way.

'Our names are easy too,' said Kewal. 'All the men are called Singh and all the women are called Kaur.'

Several of the group laughed in a fashion that told Nicky that it was an old joke. A high, imperious voice croaked from the hand-cart.

'My grandmother does not speak English,' explained Kewal as the big man turned and began a conversation in the strange language. Nicky realized that all the talk about the canary had been in English for her sake. The woman who had been dabbing at her knees rose and took her hand and started to clean the grazes.

'How is your head?' said a voice at her side. 'I regret that I had to hit you so forcibly.'

She turned and saw the fat man who had first spoken to

her. He was smiling nervously. His eyes had the look of a dog's which thinks it may have done something bad but doesn't want you to think so.

'My uncle is very quick and strong,' said Kewal. 'Although he does not look it.'

There was another little laugh among the group. Nicky felt her cheek.

'It's all right,' she said. 'It's still a bit sore but it's all right. It doesn't matter, Mr – er – Singh?'

Her voice turned the last two words into a question. She knew that Kewal had been joking, but she didn't know what the joke was. However, the fat man smiled and nodded. The old voice creaked another order. You could hear it quite plainly through the chatter of the rest of the group.

'Come,' said Kewal. 'My grandmother wishes to speak to you.'

The old woman was still just as terrifying as before. She lay on her elbow on the cushions and stared. She wore about five necklaces, and every finger of her left hand had at least two rings on it. Nicky wanted to propitiate her, to make her less fierce and strange, so without taking her eyes from the many-wrinkled face she began to grope in her satchel. The old woman spoke – two sentences – and the big man laughed.

'My mother is pleased with you,' he said. 'She says you fight well, like a Sikh. But now you must fight for us, and not against.'

Nicky's fingers found what she wanted. She walked right up to the cart.

'Would you like this?' she said, giving a little half-curtsey: the old woman might be a witch, but she was a queen too. Nicky put the gold-and-coral necklace down on a blue satin cushion. The ringed claw picked it up and the bright eyes examined it, stone by stone. The old woman clucked, spoke again and put it down on the cushion.

'My mother is grateful,' said the big man. 'She says it is good gold and well-carved beads, but you must keep the necklace. You are to help us and we are to help you, so there is no need for an exchange of gifts. We will protect you, and share our food and drink with you. In return you will warn us if we seem to you to be embarking on anything which is dangerous, or wrong. Things like Kewal starting the engine of that bus. Do you understand?'

Nicky tore her eyes at last from the old woman's.

'Yes, Mr Singh,' she said, more confidently this time.

The big man's lips moved into a smile under his dark grey beard.

'You will have to learn our other names too, you know,' he said. 'Now we must march on. You will walk with my sister's family. Neena!'

Nicky picked the necklace off the blue cushion. She was glad she hadn't had to give it away.

2

FIRST NIGHT

NEENA, the big man's sister, was a dark little woman, only two or three inches taller than Nicky.

'You may put your satchel into my pram,' she said. 'I expect you are very tired.'

She spoke so softly that Nicky could hardly hear her. She looked tired and worried herself. A sulky baby sat in the pram, almost hidden by a hill of bundles.

'Thank you,' said Nicky, and propped the satchel on the handles of the pram, leaning it against the bundles. Then she found she was still holding the lemonade-bottle which she'd taken out to fight with, so she unscrewed the top and started to drink. The lemonade was nastily sweet and warm, and very fizzy with the shaking it had had, so that the froth bubbled back into her nose and made her sneeze; through her snortings she heard the boy in the pram begin a slow wail.

'Oh dear,' said Nicky, 'is that my fault?'

'He is thirsty,' said Neena, 'and we cannot spare much water because we have to boil it all.'

She leaned her light weight against the handles to get the pram going as the rest of the group moved off. Nicky, walking beside her, felt in the satchel for another bottle and handed it to Neena. The baby was watching; its wail softened to a snivel.

'No,' said Neena, 'it is yours. You will need it.'

'I can easily break into another pub,' said Nicky. 'That's how I got these.'

Neena looked at her doubtfully for a moment.

'Thank you, Nicky,' she said. 'Push the pram please, Gopal.'

A boy about Nicky's size took the handles and started to shove while Neena rummaged in her bundles for a mug; she filled it from the lemonade bottle and tilted it carefully to the baby's lips. The baby put up a hand to steady it, but did not help much; still, Neena managed very cleverly despite having to glide beside the pram.

'My brother is nicer than this, really,' said Gopal, 'but he knows that something is wrong and that my mother is worried.'

'Are you really all called Singh?' said Nicky in a half-whisper.

'Yes. It was an order of the guru three hundred years ago that all Sikhs are called Singh. It means "lion", and we are a soldier people.'

He spoke very proudly and seriously.

'What are Sikhs?' said Nicky.

'We are Sikhs. My people are Indians – Indian Indians, of course, not American Indians – but many of us came to England, especially after the war. We have a different religion from you and from other Indians and we carry five signs that we are different. Other Indians wear the turban, for instance, but we do not cut our hair or beards at all, ever; we carry a sword to show we are soldiers; we wear a steel bracelet; we . . .'

'I can't see any swords,' said Nicky, who had been puzzled by the explanation. She felt that she ought to know about the war, and about Indians, just as she ought to have known about turbans, but she'd forgotten. She was irritated by being forced to recognize another of those moments when she saw or heard something which felt as though she'd dreamed it before, but had forgotten the dream.

Gopal laughed and felt in the back of his turban. From it he produced a square wooden comb to which was fastened a toy scimitar two inches long.

'You cannot wear a sword if you are working in a bank,' he said, 'or driving a train in the underground. Not a real killing sword. So we wear our swords like this, but they are still a sign of our faith and a sign that we are a soldier people. We are a very proud race, you know. When a man joins the Sikh religion he becomes taller and stronger and braver. It has often happened. I have read it in my history books.'

'How old are you?' said Nicky.

'Thirteen.'

'I'm twelve. Shall I help you push the pram or are you too proud?'

He laughed again, as though he was used to being teased and didn't mind. His face was thin and his skin looked silky-soft; he moved his brown eyes about a lot when he spoke or listened, in a way that was full of meanings. Nicky decided that she liked him, but that he was a bit girlish. It was only later that she found he was a true lion, worthy of his name.

'You can help me up the next hill,' he said. 'We will give my mother a rest.'

Neena – Mrs Singh or Mrs Kaur, Nicky decided she ought to call her – turned her weary face to smile at her son, then started to arrange the bundles on the pram so that the little boy could sleep.

In fact the next hill was a long time coming. Castelnau is a flat mile from end to end, between friendly Victorian mansions; then it bends and become Ranelagh Gardens, quaintly ornate red houses with little unusable balconies crowding all down one side, and on the other a six-foot wooden fence

screening Barn Elms Park from the traffic. Ranelagh Gardens
twists to cross the miniature scrub desert of Barnes Common. (Here a bedraggled horse stumbled out of the bushes
and followed them, until one of the rear-guard tried to
catch it and it shied away.)

On the far side of the Common the road humps itself up
over a railway. Nicky fulfilled her bargain by toiling beside
Gopal to heave the pram up to the ridge of the hummock,
but she could only just manage it, so much of her strength
had the rage of her fight taken. On the bridge some of the
children crowded to the wall and gossiped in English about
the odd little station with its lace-like fringes of fretted
wood, until angry voices called them back to the line of
march. Down the far slope a pram ran away from its pusher
and was caught amid excited shouts by the advance-guard.
(It seemed to Nicky that the shouting and the excitement
were much more than were needed for an ordinary pram
trundling down hill with nobody in it, only bundles and
cardboard boxes.)

The long climb up Roehampton Lane was another matter.
Ropes and straps were produced and tied to every cart and
pram, so that two could pull and one could push. The men
in the rear-guard and advance-guard had to do their share as
well, but they pulled with one hand while the other held
their thick staves ready over their shoulders. Neena returned
to the handles of the pram and Nicky and Gopal each took
a strap. It didn't seem hard work for the first few steps, but
as the wide road curved endlessly upwards Nicky began to
stagger with weariness. Nobody spoke. The iron rims of the
cartwheels crunched on the tarmac, and the eighty feet
padded or scraped according to how they were shod. Nicky
bent her head and hauled, seeing nothing but the
backward-sliding road beneath her, hearing nothing but the

thin whistle of her breath in her throat. She stumbled, and stumbled again.

As she was still reeling from the daze of her second stumble she heard the old woman's voice creak, and a man shouted, 'Ho, Kaka, you fat villain, give the English girl a rest and work off some of your grease by pulling on a rope.'

Nicky looked up hopefully. A roly-poly boy about eight years old came and held out his hand for the strap.

'Please,' he said shyly.

'This is my cousin Kaka,' said Gopal from the other side of the pram. 'I have twenty-seven cousins, and Kaka is the worst.'

Kaka smiled through his shyness as though Gopal had been paying him a compliment, and immediately gave such a sturdy lug at the strap that the pram shot sideways across the procession and Neena locked wheels with the pram next door. Even the weary women laughed as they scolded Kaka, and the men halted and leaned on their staves to watch the fun.

The march only stopped for a couple of minutes, but it felt like a proper rest. Nicky walked beside Gopal on the other side of the pram. It was interesting to see how warily the leading men looked into every driveway and turning as they went past, and how often the others glanced from side to side or looked over their shoulders, as though every garden of the whole blind and silent suburb might hide an ambush.

'Is everybody here your relation?' she said.

'No,' said Gopal. 'Daya Wanti – that is the old lady on the cart – is my grandmother, and she has four sons and two daughters. My mother is the youngest. All my uncles and aunts have married, and they have children. Some of the children are grown up, like my cousin Kewal and my cousin Punam, who washed your knees; and then my father has a sister who is married and has children, and there is a family who are relations of the lady who married my Uncle Chacha Rahmta. You think that is a funny name, I expect.'

'Well, er,' said Nicky.

'It is a funny name, in English,' said Gopal.

'I expect Nicola Gore is a funny name in some languages,' said Nicky.

'Oh, yes, I assure you that in Eskimo language Nicola Gore means ... means ... bother, I can't think of anything silly enough.'

'Oak-tree soup,' said Nicky.

'The Eskimos do not have oak trees.'

'That's why they chose a silly word for oak-tree soup. Which is Mr Chacha Rahmta?'

'He is the one who knocked you over.'

'But everybody here is your relation or married one of your relations or something like that?'

'No, not quite. We have some friends who have come alone from India and decided to live near us. When the madness happened to all the English people, they gathered to us for safety. You do not mind me talking about the madness? That is what we call it.'

'I expect so,' said Nicky without thinking about it. 'Is your grandmother the chief?'

'Oh, no. The women have an equal voice with the men, and of course the voice of the older people is more respected than the voice of the younger people; but we all decide together what to do, and then . . .'

'And then my mother tells us what we are going to do despite that,' interrupted a man from Nicky's other side. It was Uncle Chacha, pulling steadily on a rope which was tied to a hand-cart laden with cardboard cartons. As he spoke the old woman screeched from her cart and the whole party stopped as if she had been a sergeant-major calling 'Halt!'

'You see what I mean?' said Uncle Chacha.

They had reached the ridge of the hill. Ahead the road dipped and curved into the small valley of Roehampton Village, and then rose almost at once towards Putney Heath and Wimbledon Common. But behind, all the roof-tiles were below them, mile upon lifeless mile, spreading right across the Thames Valley and up the far northern hills. Perhaps a few hundred people were still living among those millions of rooms, eating what they could scavenge, like rats in a stable; otherwise it was barren as a desert, just long dunes of bricks and cement and slate and asphalt. Far to the east something big was burning, where a huge ragged curve of smoke tilted under the mild wind.

The Sikhs broke into their clattering gossip even before they settled for their rest. The children were too tired now for running-about games, but pointed and badgered their elders about the cluster of high-rise flats which stood close to the road, like the broken pillars of some temple of the giants. The baby in the pram woke, and was lifted out to totter around on the pavement. The adults sat along a low wall, and passed bottles of water from hand to hand, from which each drank a few sips. Nicky felt thirsty again, but didn't dare start her last bottle for fear of making the baby cry. Perhaps if she moved further away . . .

Down in the dip, right in the middle of the village, was a pub. She stood up and trotted down the hill. A voice cried after her, but she waved her hand without looking round, to show that she knew what she was doing. The rosebed in the forecourt of the pub was edged with tilted bricks; she prised one out and used it to hammer at the pane of frosted glass which was the top half of the door; the glass clashed and tinkled as it fell to the floor inside. The first blow was the dangerous one, because the glass might go anywhere; after that, if you were sensible, it was quite easy to knock away the jagged lengths of pane around the central hole, until you were tapping away the last sharp splinters along the wooden rim at the bottom.

That done, Nicky took her spare skirt out of her satchel and laid it along the wood; she put her hands on the skirt, bounced twice on her toes to get the feel of the ground, and flicked herself neatly through the gap. Gym had been her best subject, once.

The saloon bar was the usual mess, with all the glasses smashed and empty bottles of beer and wine and whisky littering the floor. The room reeked of stale drink. But, as usual, the men who had roared and rioted in here a month ago had not been interested in the soft drinks, except as things to throw and fight with; there were several crates of ginger ale and lemonade and tonic water under the bar counter. She heaved one out and started to drag it to the door. The light changed; there was a crash and a thump behind her; Gopal, her friend from the pram, was sprawling across the floor, gasping and giggling, his feet still scuffling among the smashed splinters.

'Are you all right?' said Nicky. 'Don't cut yourself.'

'I am less good at jumping than you are,' he said, turning round to look at the door while he brushed his trousers with his hands. 'If we turn your crate on its end we will be able to unbolt the door. Then we can drag your loot out.'

But outside the door stood Uncle Chacha, looking serious. Kewal, the young man she had tried to kill, was lounging up behind him, while Neena watched anxiously from half way down the slope.

'You are a bad little boy, Gopal,' said Uncle Chacha. 'You must not wander away like this. Your mother is very worried.'

Probably he spoke in English so that Nicky could share in the reproof.

'It's quite safe,' she said. 'We're only getting some lemonade for the children.'

(She didn't tell him about the pub she'd broken into north of Shepherd's Bush where a dead man had sat, sprawled across a shiny red table, with a knife in his side.)

'It is notorious that Indian parents over-protect their children,' said Kewal. 'But that is what they do, Miss Nicky Gore, and you must respect their anxieties.'

'All right,' said Nicky. 'Will you help us with the crate? There's plenty for everybody.'

'But we cannot take this,' said Uncle Chacha slowly. 'It is not our property.'

'It isn't anybody's,' said Nicky. 'They've all gone.'

'We could put some money in the till,' suggested Kewal. 'It's smashed,' said Gopal. 'I noticed.'

Uncle Chacha walked into the pub, very careful and light on his feet, like a wild animal sniffing into a trap. He counted five green pieces of paper into a broken drawer. Kewal waved to the crowd on the hill and they gathered themselves into line of march and trooped down to the pub. Kewal explained what had happened, and half-a-dozen angry voices answered him, all together. Several faces looked at Nicky. The women joined in the row. Suddenly something was settled and four of the men went into the pub to fetch more crates, and tins of peanuts and crisps and cheese biscuits. The whole party settled to an impromptu picnic. The children recovered strength and began a squealing game of chain he. The towers of empty flats brooded silent in the dusty afternoon air. The men settled into one group, and the women into another. Every half minute a mother would look up from her gossip and call to a child in words that Nicky couldn't understand, but in the tone that all mothers everywhere use when they are warning their children to be careful. Nicky, all of a sudden, felt just as lonely and left out as she had that morning on the Green, before the Sikhs had come.

'Do you not wish to join the game,' said Kewal, who had appeared silently beside her. 'Are you too old for that sort of thing, perhaps? Look, Gopal is playing.'

'I'm too tired and hot,' said Nicky, sighing to keep the crossness out of her voice. 'What's the name of the language you talk among yourselves?'

'Punjabi. It is the normal language of the Sikhs, although some of the children who have lived all their lives here find English easier to talk. I myself think in English, even when I am talking Punjabi.'

'Why are you all still here? Why did you leave so late? Everybody else went away a long time ago.'

'Oh,' said Kewal, 'at first we could not decide what was happening. Some of us used to work for London Transport, but when the early shift went to get the buses out they were attacked by mobs of Englishmen. Even the little children threw stones as soon as an engine started. And they were not like you – they did not stop when the engines were turned off. Perhaps it was because there were many of them; it is difficult you know, for a whole crowd to stop rioting once they have started. But none of my relations was killed, though my cousin Surbans Singh was badly beaten. So they came home, and the rest of us could not go to work because none of the buses and trains was running. I started to bicycle to University – I am a student – but I was chased by shouting people so I came home too. We shut ourselves in our houses (we have three houses all together in the same road) and held a council. We decided that all the English people had been infected by a madness against machines, which for some reason did not affect us Sikhs. Oh, now I will tell you something interesting and significant. The Jamaicans also had gone to get the buses out, but my cousin Surbans said that they were extremely clumsy and giggled all the time when they made a mistake. He thought they had all been drinking – at four o'clock in the morning, which is not impossible with Jamaicans. So perhaps they too were a little affected by the madness, but not in the same manner as the English. Anyway our council decided that we would wait until the madness passed. But it did not pass. One of my uncles owns a store, so there was enough to eat, but water became difficult and sanitary arrangements too. And it was difficult to cook without . . . What is the matter, Miss Gore?'

Nicky had only been able to understand about half of what Kewal said. His explanation seemed full of nasty, fuzzy words and ideas, such as 'bicycle'. She felt a qualm of the old sick rage bubbling up inside her – the rage she'd felt in Castelnau, or on that first morning when Daddy had gone round the house with his hammer smashing all the nasty gadgets of their lost life. But it was only a qualm this time, not strong enough for killing or smashing. She put her head between her hands and waited for the qualm to seep away. Kewal watched her in silence.

'Please don't talk about things like that,' she said at last. 'You mustn't.'

'Why?'

'I don't know why, but you mustn't.'

He smiled.

'You are a good canary,' he said. 'You will be most useful to us. I must go and tell my uncles what you say.'

'No, wait,' said Nicky. 'I think I can explain a bit more. Gopal was talking to me before, and he said things which worried me in a different kind of way. The things you were talking about made me feel very angry, very mad really. I don't mind your calling it madness, because it's just like that. But Gopal was talking about India, and the war and things which I'm sure I knew about once. But now it's ... it's as if they'd become so . . . so *boring*. I suppose, that my brain goes to sleep before I can think about them. I couldn't remember the word for your hats until he told me it was "turbans". Do you understand?'

'Aha!' said Kewal, his terrible squint sparkling with pleasure at his own cleverness. 'I begin to see. Shall I explain my theorem to you?'

'No, please,' said Nicky, who had only just managed to struggle through the discomfort of trying to think about the shut places of her own mind. 'Go and tell your uncles.'

That caused further delay while the two groups of grown-ups joined to discuss Nicky; at one point a quarrel broke out and excitable fists were flung skywards, but it was all over as suddenly as a child's tantrums. Then at last they were on the march again, hauling prams and carts up the steep slope to the Common, then turning right to trundle down towards Kingston. The children who had darted so eagerly through their game became tired almost at once, oppressed by the dreariness of the slow walk. By the time they came to Robin Hood roundabout, where the road divides, one of the smallest ones was snivelling and several mothers had found space for an extra burden on their prams. Nicky helped fat Kaka up on to the old lady's cart.

'I shall not be able to push a great weight like yours except downhill,' said the big man severely. Kaka grinned between fat cheeks and reached for his grandmother's hand. Or perhaps she was his great-grandmother, Nicky thought. All the grown-ups seemed to show a special kindness towards the small children, despite their strange fierce looks.

At the roundabout a further conference was held. Nicky lounged amid the incomprehensible babble and looked north, through Robin Hood Gate, to where the green reaches of Richmond Park lay quiet in the westering sun.

'Miss Gore,' a voice called. It was the big uncle.

'Yes.'

'We are discussing whether we should go through Kingston or along the by-pass. It is shorter to go through, although there is a big hill. Would it, shall I say, *affect* you if we went one way or the other?'

'I don't know,' said Nicky. 'Couldn't we go in there?'

She pointed to the inviting greenness of the Park. Some of

the mothers made approving noises. The discussions in Punjabi clattered out again. Really, Nicky couldn't understand how any of them could be *listening* with so many of them talking all together. This time the women seemed to have more to say than the men, but at last the noise quietened and in the lull Gopal's grandmother said something decisive. The march wheeled into the Park.

'We have decided that the children have gone far enough,' said Neena, 'so we shall camp here for the night. The women wanted to sleep in a house, but the men said there was more danger of sickness. My mother said that we shall have to camp often, and this would be a warm fine night, with no enemies about, to practise.'

'Oh, this is much nicer than houses,' said Nicky.

The grass stood tall, shivering in faint slow waves under a breeze so slight that it seemed to be the sunlight itself that moved the stems. The copses looked cool and dark. A cackle of interest burst from several lips together; following the pointing arms Nicky saw a troop of deer move out of shade into sunlight. The big uncle studied his map and led the march right-handed to where a swift brook flowed in a banked channel.

Here, while a dozen mothers scolded children in Punjabi about the dangers of falling in, they began to set up camp slowly, arguing about every detail, four people fussing over some easy matter while a fifth struggled alone with an unmanageable load. The fifth might shout angrily for help, but his voice went unnoticed amid the clamour.

Then, quite suddenly, everything was sorted out to everyone's satisfaction and the women started to fill pots from the stream while the men and the older boys straggled off towards the nearest copse.

'You come too, Nicky,' called Gopal.

Half way to the trees they came to a neat stack of fencing-posts which the men picked up and carried back to the stream while the boys and Nicky went on.

'That was a bit of luck,' said Gopal. 'Now we shall have a first-rate fire if we can find some kindling-wood.'

Nicky was struck again by something that had been puzzling her about the way Gopal and the others spoke. The children didn't have the slightly sing-song lilt of the grown-up Sikhs, but the actual words they used were oddly exact and careful, and if Gopal said something slangy the slang would seem a little quaint and old-fashioned – like 'first-rate'.

As they reached the edge of the wood they heard a scuffling and snorting, and about twenty deer flounced away uphill, then turned to watch them from beyond throwing range.

'If only I had a gun!' said one of the older boys with a laugh. 'Pow! Wump! Kerzoingg!'

'No!' cried Nicky.

'A bow and arrow, perhaps,' said Gopal in a teasing voice.

'Yes, that would be all right,' said Nicky, seriously.

It took them some time to gather dry twigs and branches and pile them together for dragging down to the camp. By then the men had fetched the whole pile of fencing-posts and were sawing them into short logs. Soon four neat fires were sending invisible flames into the strong, slant sun. Pots boiled. Some of the men were cutting bracken up the hill, others were rigging a mysterious screen. A child fell into the stream, but luckily Kewal was sitting on the bank, brooding at the passing water, and he snatched it out. The child was scolded for falling in and Kewal for not doing his share of the work. Nicky half-dozed, and wondered whether it was all a dream.

'Come and wash, Nicky,' said Neena. 'If you want to.'

There was nothing she wanted more. The women were queueing to wash behind the screen, using barely more than a mugful of hot water each in a collapsible canvas baby-bath. Nicky, ashamed at her month's grime, used more than her share of water, but nobody complained. Cousin Punam inspected her scratches and dabbed some nasty-smelling stuff along the sore place where her collar had been rubbing. Neena borrowed clothes for her from another mother. Then she joined the chattering laundry-party.

A frowning woman, darker than the others and with flecks of grey in her hair, hung out her own clothes beside Nicky and looked at her several times without speaking.

'We Sikhs are a very clean people,' she said at last, in an accusing voice. 'We are cleaner than Europeans.'

'I like being clean too,' said Nicky.

'Good,' said the woman without smiling.

Then Nicky was called over to where the men, who had also been washing and laundering, were holding a council. Gopal had told them about the gun and the bow, and now they settled down to ask her random questions about what they could or could not do with safety. It was difficult because some of the questions made her sick and unhappy again; besides, the way they all asked different questions at the same time, or started discussions in Punjabi among themselves, or became involved in flaring arguments about things that didn't seem to matter at all – all this muddled her attempts at sensible answers. If she hadn't been so tired she would have laughed at them several times, but soon she realized that it wouldn't have been a good idea. They were too proud and prickly to take kindly to being laughed at by an outsider. She thought they wouldn't actually hurt her, not now; but looking at the rich beards and the strong teeth and the dark eyes, fiery and secret, she was sure that they could be very cruel to their enemies.

And Nicky wasn't an enemy – but she was determined not to be a friend either. As the big uncle had said, she was to help them and they were to help her, but one day that would end, and it must end without hurting her. She realized that her raid on the pub had been partly a way of saying that she didn't belong, that the Sikhs had no other claims on her than the single contract of alliance. She was their canary, but she was neither friend nor enemy.

While one of the longest arguments straggled on, Nicky noticed a movement just beyond the group. Four or five deer, long accustomed to the idea that people mean picnickers, and picnickers mean scraps of food, had come nosing up. Uncle Chacha, who hadn't spoken as much as the others so far, now broke into the argument in Punjabi, shifting a couple of feet back out of the circle as he did so. The deer shied away at his movement, then drifted slowly in again.

'Do not look at them, Miss Gore,' said one of the Uncles. 'A wild animal is made more nervous by the gaze of the hunter.'

'I do wish everyone would call me Nicky,' she said. 'Miss Gore sounds like somebody's aunt.'

Smiles glowed amid the beards.

'Okay,' said several voices; but they said it quietly, and when the discussion rambled on it did so without any sudden bursts of shouting which might disturb a wild animal.

She never saw Uncle Chacha strike because she was carefully not looking straight at the deer. But in the corner of her eye there was a flash of movement, a silent explosion followed by one sharp thud. Then the deer were bounding away and all the Sikhs were on their feet, crowding round and cheering. Nicky jostled through to see what had happened and found Uncle Chacha standing, stave in hand, by what looked like a pale brown sack. He hung his head with exactly Kaka's shyness – he must be the fat boy's father.

Then Nicky saw that the sack had a spindly leg, and a round eye big as a halfpenny, dull and unwinking.

'He broke its neck with his lathi,' said Kewal proudly. 'One blow, bim, like that. We will have roast venison for supper.'

The council was over. Nicky raced twigs on the stream with Gopal and his friends for a bit, then joined in a game of blind man's buff. Then all the children sat in a circle round the cart to hear the old lady tell them a story, so Nicky went off to play with a tiny brown baby, Neena's niece, which kicked and gurgled on a pink towel. After that she curled up and slept amid the tickling grasses.

It was almost dark when they woke her, and the dewy dusk smelt beautifully of roasted meat. They all sat on the trampled grass in a ragged circle round the fires; even the smallest babies were awake again, staring from their mothers' laps at the wavering flames. The Sikhs looked stranger still as the night deepened; the men's beards became like huge shadows – shadows with no shape to cast them – and in these shadows a row of teeth would gleam for a moment when a mouth opened to talk or smile or chew; the eyes too shone weird in the weird light. They looked like a ring of pirates, murderous invaders.

The venison was charred at the edges and tough to chew, but full of delicious juices even if you did have to spit out the pithy gobbets of fibre that were left unswallowable at the end of each mouthful. The Sikhs had made a curry sauce to dip the meat into, and passed it round in pots, but it was too hot for Nicky. The grown-ups ate a flattish scone-like bread called chapattis, which they'd brought with them, but the children preferred to finish off the crisps from the pub. The drinking-water was still tepid from its boiling, but delicious after a month of lemonade.

When they'd finished eating, the big man stood up by the old lady's cart and read in a solemn voice from a book. Sometimes the Sikhs answered him, all together.

'Prayers,' whispered Gopal in Nicky's ear.

Some of the babies were asleep again before he'd finished, and now they were settled into their prams. An awning had been built over the old lady's cart, and the cut bracken piled into mounds under that and the other carts for the smeller children to sleep on. The older children and the grown-ups slept in the open, women and girls in one group, men and boys in the other. Somebody had a spare blanket to lend Nicky. The bracken was surprisingly comfortable.

'You see?' said Neena as they were sorting themselves out. 'It takes a long time to make a camp. It is a lot of hard work. We cannot hope to march more than ten miles a day, with the children to think about and the carts and prams to push.'

'Where are you going to?' said Nicky.

'We do not know. We will just go until we find a place where we can live. Perhaps it is across the sea, but I hope not.'

3

GOOD LAND, CLEAN WATER

A PLACE where they could live.

They came to it eight days later, but did not recognize it at first. They thought it was just a sensible place to stop for a few days so that Rani, Neena's sister-in-law, could have her baby. On the left of the lane stood a raw, ugly, square brick farmhouse with metal-frame windows; then, a little further up the hill, was a brick shed; then a tiny brand-new bungalow; and then, for them to camp in, an old brick farmyard built like a fort with a single gateway, an old barn down one side, and on the others single-storey cattle-sheds and grain-stores. A hundred yards on, right on the ridge of the hill, loomed two vast new asbestos-and-concrete barns and a cluster of grain-towers. On the other side of the lane there was only a single house, opposite the farmyard; it had once been two old cottages for farm labourers, but someone had run them together and smartened them up for an artist to live in.

He'd gone, and so had all the other people. Every house was empty. No cattle lowed for milking, no cat miaowed on any doorstep. Hundreds of birds clattered in the hedges round the artist's cottage, but the farmer had hauled out every other hedge on his land to make it easier to cultivate the flowing steppes of hay and wheat and barley that now stood rippling in the upland wind across six hundred acres.

A mile and a half down the hill you could see the tower of Felpham Church, warm brick, rising amid limes, seeming to move nearer when the afternoon sun shone full on it, and then to drift away when a cloud-shadow hid the sun. You could see only a few roofs of Felpham, although it was quite a big village. Beyond that was distance.

And the distance really was distance, although the farm stood barely a hundred and fifty feet above the plain which stretched to the north east. For twenty miles there was nothing else as high. There were no real landmarks, except the now useless pylons. A double row of these swooped across the slope between the farm and the village, but Nicky tried not to see them. Instead she gazed out beyond them to the mottled leagues, blue and grey and green, that reached towards London. She felt that she could still count every footstep of the road they had come.

It was the people that she remembered most. First the old tramp who had come, snuffling like a hedgehog, up to their camp on Esher Common and asked for food. The Sikhs had simply made room for him, dirty as he was, and fed him all he wanted. He must have been half-crazy, for he seemed to notice no difference between them and other people, nor between these times and other times, but just mumbled and chewed, and at last lurched away into the dark without a word of thanks.

But the first real people they'd met — ordinary English people, wearing English clothes — had been at Ripley. And they'd been enemies. A dozen men and women had run out of a pub at the sound of the iron wheels on the road. For a while they'd simply stared as the march of Sikhs moved slowly past, but one of the women had said something mocking to the men, then a man had shouted and all the men were throwing stones and bottles at the Sikhs while the women cursed and jeered. Kaka had been hit by a stone, but had managed not to cry. Nicky had dashed from the line, shouting to the men to stop it; their attitude changed, and for a moment she'd thought they'd heard her and understood, until the rear-guard of the Sikhs rushed past her, staves whirling. The Englishmen had broken and run, while their women cowered against the wall. As the procession moved out of Ripley there were catcalls from behind walls, and clods of earth lobbed into the line, but no one had followed them. And the people working in the fields paid no attention as they marched by, grim and silent.

They'd camped that night in a field north of Guildford, on the banks of the river Wey, and had held another council. The discussion sounded earnest and subdued, and after it a party of men had gone night-raiding into Guildford, though there'd still seemed to be plenty of food left in the cardboard boxes on the carts. (Seeing a tin opened made Nicky uneasy, but the meat inside tasted all right.)

They'd decided to head for the coast, but to avoid towns and villages even if it meant going the long way round. However, the houses in the Home Counties are so closesown that you're bound to pass some of them, and at the very next hamlet two or three faces had leaned out of windows and called cheerily for news, just as though columns of bearded foreigners passed that way so often that there was nothing strange about it. So for a while they'd felt more optimistic, but as they steadily trudged the days away they'd learnt that every village was different, and that the frowning ones were commoner than the smiling ones. And people seemed to have little idea of what was happening more than a mile or two from their own doors.

No more stones were thrown at them, but they had thrown some themselves. This was in their second battle, on the outskirts of Aldershot, a much nastier business than the skirmish at Ripley. The enemy had been a wandering gang

of robbers, though at first they'd looked like another procession, trundling down the sunk road towards the Sikhs;
but almost at once a dozen young men armed with pick-
helves had charged shouting and yelling, forcing the Sikhs'
advance guard back against the group of women and children. Uncle Chacha had brought the rear-guard up in a
counter-attack. While the grunts and bellows rose Nicky
stared wildly round for something she could do. Gopal
grabbed her elbow and pointed to the flinty chalk at the top
of the embankment, and the next moment they were
scrambling desperately up. There'd been seven of the children up there, screaming and hurling flints, by the time
the robbers broke and ran back to where four or five dirty
women had been watching the fun from among their own
prams and barrows. The angry Sikhs had driven the lot of
them on down the road, hitting as hard as they could. Nicky

had stopped to look at the robbers' baggage, which had turned out to be a hoard of cheap looted jewellery, a lot of boxes of sweets and some mouldy loaves. The Sikhs left it all where it was.

Mr Gurchuran Singh had hurt his leg in the battle, so they'd decided to rest for a couple of days where they next found water. They had posted extra sentries that night, and after supper the big uncle, whose name was Mr Jagindar Singh, had spoken very earnestly to Nicky.

'We think you should leave us,' he said, 'as soon as we next come to friendly people. You will be safer with them than with us. We propose to try to reach the sea and go away to France. We listened to the Paris radio in London, and they are free from this madness there.'

'But what will you do for a canary?' Nicky had said.

'Oh, we shall be careful. You have taught us much.'

'I'd rather come with you for a bit longer, Mr Singh.'

'We do not consider it wise.'

'What does your mother say?'

'Ha, you have bewitched her, Nicky. She says that it is no business of ours, and that you are to make up your own mind.'

Nicky had looked towards the cushioned cart and seen the bird-bright eyes watching her through the gloom.

'Please then,' she'd said, 'I'd much rather stay. I don't want to have to learn to know a *new* lot of people. Have you still got the ... the thing you listened to France with?'

'Kaka knocked it off the table and none of us knew how to mend it.'

'Good.'

She'd meant what she'd said about the new people. They would be English, like her, and the kindlier they were the worse it would be, day after day probing to pierce through the clumsy armour she'd built round her heart. They would try to be mothers, and fathers, and perhaps even the sisters and brothers she had never had. And only she would know, all the time, in waking nightmares as well as the deeps of dream, how such a home can be smashed in a single morning. She couldn't live through that again.

Besides, against all her reason, she had made a new

friend. Kaka's elder sister Ajeet was a very quiet girl whom Nicky had at first thought was seven or eight; in fact the two of them had been born only a week apart, though on opposite sides of the world. They had fallen into that instant, easy friendship which feels as though it had begun before any of your memories and will last until you are so old that the humped veins on the back of your hands show dark blue-purple through your wax-white skin. Ajeet's mother — Uncle Chacha's wife — was the fat frowning woman, and she seemed anxious to know about every breath her children drew, but they all seemed happy enough when you got to know them. At least she didn't try to be a mother to Nicky.

They had to move before Mr Gurchuran Singh's leg was properly healed, because a passing horseman had shouted to them that there was plague in Aldershot. That had meant a long journey round the northern edge of that ugly, shambling town, so in the end they had come to Felpham from the north, taking eight days to get there from London. Felpham was a frowning village, but not a stone-throwing one, so they had trudged through and begun the long push up Strake Lane, never guessing that they were nearly home. In fact Nicky almost refused to pass the double line of pylons, because they seemed so much worse than the single ones which she'd crossed with a slight shudder before, but Gopal cajoled her under.

It had rained twice that day, and there were looming clouds about, so they were glad of the farmyard roofs and the dry hay beneath them. Four of the men pushed a cart laden with pots to Strake, two miles further along the road. There was a pond marked on the map at Strake.

It was Nicky who found the old well, which had enabled the farm to be built there in the first place. The close eye which the Sikh parents kept on their children irked her, though she didn't like to say so, but she tended to drift off and explore as soon as she had done what she could to help set up camp; it was her way of saying that she wasn't going to let herself be watched and pampered like that. Once or twice Gopal had slipped away and come with her, only to be scolded when they got back, but this time she was alone.

The artist's cottage was locked. Nose against windows, Nicky could see a low-ceilinged kitchen and another big room which had been made by knocking down several walls. Light streamed into it through a big skylight in the far roof. She didn't feel like visiting the huge barns because they'd be full of engines, and everywhere else was nothing but rippling wheat; so she sat on a low circular flint wall, topped with a line of brick, and thought about nothing much. The shouting and chatter of the encampment washed over her unheeded. The centre of the flint wall was covered with a four-foot round of wood; she thought vaguely that it must be some sort of garden table, uncomfortable because you couldn't get your knees under it. She slapped the timber with her palm.

A slow boom answered, as though the whole hill were speaking, the million-year-old chalk answering her knock in tones almost too deep to hear. Each slap or rap produced the same bass reply. She got her fingers under the edge of the wood and it came up like a lid.

The hole in the centre of the circle was black. It was a tunnel of night defying the gay sun. The palms of her hands went chilly as she clutched the brick rim and peered in. At first she could see nothing, but then there was a faint light, a circle of sky with a head and shoulders in the middle. The rough chalk walls dwindled down, becoming invisible in darkness before they reached the water. She dropped a stone but it fell crooked, clacking several times from wall to wall before the splash. She went to fetch Kewal.

He dropped three or four stones, with his other hand feeling his pulse. Even when the stones fell straight it seemed ages before the splash answered.

'About fifty feet to the water,' he said. 'If we can get it up, and if the water is good, it means we can stay here for a while. The women say that Rani's baby will be born in two or three days.'

They found a rope and bucket in the sheds, but it took a lot of trial and error and a lot of many-voiced arguments before the men rigged up a method of getting a bucket down all that distance and making it lie sideways when it reached the water, so that it filled, and then tilted upright when it was full. Hauling a full bucket up from fifty feet was tiring, too, but it was better than walking to Strake. And the water when it came was so sweet and clean that Cousin Punam decided it was safe to drink without boiling.

It was Gopal who found the corn. While Rani was in labour, three days later, the older children were shushed away. Nicky didn't follow them up to the big barns because she felt uncomfortable there. She was looking, with little luck, for late wild strawberries in the matted grass on the banks of the lane when Gopal came hurrying past, his hands cupped close together as if he was trying to carry water. Nicky thought he'd caught a bird and ran to look.

'Nicky, you're a ninny,' he said. 'This is *food*. I climbed an iron ladder up one of those round towers and opened a lid at the top and it is full of corn. There is enough to feed us for a year. Look, it is dry and good.'

He ran to show his treasure to the men-folk, while Nicky returned to combing through the weeds for strawberries.

She found no more of the little red globules of sweetness, but caught a grasshopper instead, let it tickle her prisoning palms for a moment, then held it free and watched it tense itself for its leap, and vanish.

The baby was born in a cow-byre. It was a boy. That night the Sikhs held full council. It was just as noisy and muddled with cross-talk as any of the ones they'd heard on the road, but Nicky got the feeling that even in the middle of rowdy arguments they were being more serious, paying more attention to what the others said. From time to time they would ask her a question.

'We cannot use any of the tractors, can we, Nicky?'

She shook her head.

'But we can reap and plough and dig and plant by hand?'

'Oh yes.'

'And there is nothing wrong with this wheat?'

'Wrong?' She looked through the gateway to where the beautiful tall blades waved, grey as fungus under the big moon, but already tinged with yellow by daylight as the year edged towards harvest.

'Oh yes,' said Mr Surbans Singh, 'this is a modern cross-bred variety of wheat, and another of barley. The madness does not apply to them, you think?'

'Oh no!'

Another long fusillade of Punjabi followed. Then . . .

'Nicky, would the madness make the villagers come and destroy us if we were to set up a blacksmith's shop?'

'What would you do?'

'Make and mend spades and sickles and ploughs and other tools.'

'I mean, how would you do it? What would you use?'

'We would have to make charcoal first, which is done by burning wood very slowly under a mound of earth. Then we would have to contrive a furnace, with bellows to keep the charcoal burning fiercely. And when the iron was red-hot we would hammer it, and bend it with vices and pincers, and then temper it in water or oil.'

'Water,' said Nicky firmly. 'Where would you get the iron from?'

'There is plenty lying around the farm.'

'I *think* that would be all right. You could try, and I could always tell you if I thought it wasn't. Why do you want to know?'

'First, because if we are to stay here we shall need hand-tools ourselves. This farm is highly mechanized, which is no doubt why the farmer left; he felt he could not work it without his tractors. But secondly, we shall need more to eat than wheat. We shall need to barter for meat and vegetables until we can produce our own. Some of us have seen smith-work done in India, in very primitive conditions; Mr Jagindar Singh was a skilled metalworker in London, and two more of us have done similar work in factories and garages; so we think we can set up an efficient smithy. But perhaps the villagers will not have our advantages, so we shall be able to barter metalwork with them in exchange for the things we need.'

'That's a good idea,' said Nicky, astonished again by the amount of sense that seemed to come out of all the clamour and repetition. 'But do you think the villagers will actually trade with you? They didn't look very friendly when we came through, and they haven't come up here at all.'

'If we make something they need, they will trade with us,' said Uncle Jagindar sombrely. 'It does not matter how much they dislike us. We have found this in other times.'

The whole council muttered agreement. Kewal gave a sharp, snorting laugh which Nicky hadn't heard before.

'We must be careful,' he said. 'If we become too rich they will want to take our wealth away from us.'

'I expect there's quite a lot of robbers in England now,' said Nicky. 'Like those ones we fought on the other side of Aldershot – men who've got no way of getting food except by robbing the ones who have.'

This set off another round of argument and discussion in Punjabi. The men seemed to become very excited; voices rose, eyes flashed, an insignificant uncle even beat his own chest. Nicky edged back out of the circle to ask Gopal what they were talking about. He was allowed at the council, but he was thought too young to speak (Nicky wouldn't have been listened to either if she hadn't been the Sikh's canary).

Gopal laughed scornfully, but he looked as excited as the rest.

'They are going to make weapons,' he said. 'Swords and spears and steel-tipped arrows. A Sikh should carry a real sword when times are dangerous. But I will tell you a joke – we Sikhs won most of our battles with guns; we used to run forward, fire a volley and then run back until we had time to reload. It does not sound very brave, but all India feared us then. What is the matter, Nicky? Oh, I'm sorry, I forgot. But they will not make guns now; instead they will turn this farmyard into a fort which we can defend against the robbers.'

After that the council became less serious, dwindling into boastings and warlike imaginings. Gopal translated the louder bits.

'My Uncle Gurchuran says we must capture horses and turn ourselves into cavalry, and then we can protect the whole countryside for a fee. A protection racket. We often lived like that in the old days . . . Mr Parnad Singh says his father was Rissaldar at an archery club in Simla, and he will teach us all to shoot. A Rissaldar is a sort of sergeant . . . My Uncle Chacha makes a joke of him and Mr Parnad Singh is angry . . . My Uncle Jagindar is trying to smooth him down; he says it will be useful to have a good shot with a bow for hunting, and that Uncle Chacha must be careful what he says, because he is so fat that he will make a first-rate target. That is unfair because Uncle Chacha is the quickest of them all, and the best fighter. You saw how he fought against those robbers . . . Now he is pretending to be angry with Uncle Jagindar, but *that* does not matter because it is inside the family . . . My grandmother is speaking. She says we must be careful how we talk to one another, because we are in a dangerous world and we cannot afford to have feuds with one another. My goodness, she says, we Sikhs are a quick-tempered people. She is beginning to tell a story. She tells very good stories, for children and adults too.'

The council had fallen silent at the creak of the old woman's voice. There had been a brief guffaw of laughter at her second sentence, but that was all. One of the men turned to glare at Gopal because his translation was spoiling the silence. He too stopped talking.

The story was not long, but the old woman told it with careful and elaborate gestures of the hands, as though she were the story-teller at some great court and had been sent for after supper to entertain the princes. Nicky could hear, even in the unknown language, that it was the story of a fierce quarrel between two proud men. She looked along the outer circle of children and saw Ajeet sitting entranced, mouth slightly parted and head craning forward as she listened and stared at the elaborate ceremony of the fluttering hands. Her lips were moving with the words, and her hands made faint unconscious efforts to flutter themselves.

All the Sikhs laughed when the story ended, then broke into smaller chattering groups. Nicky crossed to where Ajeet still sat staring at the orange firelight.

'What was the story about, Ajeet?' she said.

'Oh, I do not know,' said Ajeet in her usual near-whisper, shy and confused.

'Please tell me. I like to know anything your grandmother says. She is so . . . so special.'

'Oh, it was a tale of two Sikh brothers, farmers, whom my grandmother knew in India, and how they quarrelled over a dead pigeon, and in the end lost their farm and their wives and everything. Listen. It was like this.'

Her voice changed and strengthened. She drew her head back and sat very upright, freeing her hands for gestures. The history of that forgotten feud rolled out in vivid, exact words, each phrase underlined with just the same gesture of finger or wrist that her grandmother had used. Once or twice she hesitated over a word, and Nicky realized that she was turning familiar Punjabi into English which didn't quite fit. When she finished Nicky found herself laughing at the ridiculous disaster, just as the men had laughed, and heard more voices laughing behind her. Kewal and three of the other men had been standing round in silence to hear the same story all over again.

'Very excellent,' said Kewal, only half mocking.

One of the men called in Punjabi over his shoulder, and was answered by a pleased cackle from the open stall where the old woman lay on her cushions; she had been watching the show too. Ajeet accepted the compliments gravely, without any of her usual shyness, then took Nicky off to say good-night to the old lady.

This had become a sort of ritual for Nicky, a good-luck thing, wherever they were. They couldn't say much to each other, even with Ajeet to translate, because their lives had been so different, but somehow it ended the day on a comfortable note.

As they crossed the yard back to the shed where the women slept, Nicky looked round the firelit walls and the black-shadowed crannies. So this was home, now.

Provided nobody came to drive them out.

They settled in slowly. The bungalow had been left unlocked, and the first thing the Sikhs did was to redecorate the bedroom with rich hangings. They took their shoes off when they went into the room. Uncle Jagindar carried the old lady in when it was finished and she clucked her satisfaction, though she wanted several details changed. Nicky watched fascinated from the doorway.

'It is a place to keep our holy book,' explained Kewal. 'My family are very orthodox Sikhs. Before these troubles some of us younger ones did not treat our religion as earnestly as the elders, but now it seems more important. It will help to keep us together.'

'We'll have to use the other houses to sleep in when the winter comes,' said Nicky. 'It'll be too cold to sleep out in the sheds.'

'You are very practical-minded. That was how the English ruled India. They would go and admire the Taj Mahal, but all the time they were thinking about drains. Anyway, my uncles do not feel it proper to break into other people's houses, even if the people have gone away.'

'They'll have to in the end,' said Nicky. 'I don't mind doing the burgling, and then once the doors are open you could all come and use the houses like you are doing this one.'

Kewal laughed and pulled his glossy beard.

'That would be an acceptable compromise,' he said. 'But I think we will not tell my uncles until you have done it. I will attend and supervise, because in my opinion your techniques of burglary are a little crude.'

But you have to be crude with metal-framed windows. They fit too tight for you to be able to slide a knife or wire through to loose the catch. Nicky broke two panes, opened two windows, climbed into two musty and silent houses, and tiptoed through the dank air to unbolt two doors. The artist's cottage was full of lovely bric-a-brac – a deer-head, and straw ornaments that were made for the finials of hayricks, and Trinidadian steel drums. Kewal delightedly began to tonk out a pop-tune, but Nicky (frightened now of what she'd done) dragged him away.

And the uncles *were* cross when she told them. (She left Kewal out of her story.) But when the women found that there was an open hearth in the cottage and a big closed stove in the farmhouse, in both of which you could burn logs, they told the uncles to stop being so high-minded. Here was somewhere to bath and attend to small babies in the warm. And though the electric cookers were useless, a little bricklaying would turn the artist's drawing-room fire into a primitive but practical oven and stove for a communal kitchen.

Even so, Uncle Jagindar spoke very seriously to Nicky.

'It is difficult for us,' he said, 'if you were my child, or one of my nieces, I would punish you for this. Perhaps you are right and we will have to use these houses in winter, but you are wrong to take decisions on your own account against the wishes of us older people. If you continue to do this, then perhaps our own children will start to copy you, and then we will have to send you away. We will be sad, but we will do it.'

'I'm sorry,' said Nicky. 'My own family weren't so ... so ...'

'If your own family were more like us,' said Uncle Jagindar, 'you would not have become separated from them as you did, even though a mad priest caused a panic.'

Nicky was surprised. Ajeet was the only person she'd told about that wild Dervish who'd pranced red-eyed beside the retreating Londoners yelling about fire and brimstone; and the thunderstorm; and the hideous mass-panic; and the long, sick misery of loss. Ajeet must have told her frowning mother, who must have passed the story on. But Uncle Jagindar was being unfair – anybody could have got lost in that screaming mob.

'All right,' she said. 'I'll try not to be a bad influence.' That was her own and secret joke – Miss Calthrop at school used to talk about girls who were bad influences, but had spoilt her case by always picking on the girls who were most fun to be with. Uncle Jagindar nodded and Nicky went up across the fields to the wood to see how the charcoal-burners were getting on.

They had made an eight-foot pyramid of logs, covered them with wet bracken, and then sealed the pile in with ashes and burnt earth. Then the pile was lit by the tedious process of dropping embers down the central funnel and carefully blocking them in with straight sticks. A pock-marked man was in charge, because he had done the job in India. Nicky hardly knew him, as he was one of the Sikhs who was not related to the main families and spoke little English; but now he leaned on his spade by the water-hole he had dug and gave orders to the two men who were build-ing a second pyramid of logs.

Gopal came into the clearing with his father, shoving a hand-cart laden with more logs for the pile.

'Wouldn't it be better sense to burn the charcoal near the log-stack?' said Nicky. 'Or cut your wood from these trees here?'

'Wrong both times,' said Gopal. 'Nought out of ten. You must have seasoned wood, and we were lucky to find that big stack up by the road. And you must have water to quench the charcoal with when you take the pile to bits. If Mr Harbans Singh had not found that spring, we might have had to carry the wood all the way down to the well.'

'How long before you get any charcoal?'

'Three days, Mr Harbans says, but the first lot may not be very good. Have you finished your bow, Rissaldar?'

They all called Mr Parnad Singh Rissaldar now. It was a joke in a way, but he seemed to like it. Perhaps it reminded him of the glories of his father's Simla club. He was an older man than the others, his beard a splendid grey waterfall. He looked up from where he was whittling at a long stave and spoke in Punjabi.

'He says he might be able to make a good bow in a year's time, when he has seasoned ash, but this will be good enough to kill a man with at twenty yards. Nicky, if we found some tempered steel on the farm, would it be safe to make a bow with that?'

'I think so,' said Nicky uncertainly.

'Let's try,' said Gopal. 'There's all sorts of metal littered about the barn.'

Half way down the huge field two bright-coloured figures were working, a man in a crimson turban and a woman in an orange sari. When the children came nearer they saw that it was Mr Surbans Singh and his wife Mohindar, he scything, she raking. Mr Surbans Singh had appointed himself head farmer.

'What are you doing?' called Gopal.

Mr Surbans Singh straightened up, but his wife (whom Nicky thought the prettiest of all the Sikhs) went on tedding the grass he'd cut into a loose line.

'I found this scythe in a shed,' he said. 'It is very bad, and the hay is grown too coarse to be good feed, but poor hay will be better than none if we are to keep sheep through the winter.'

'Sheep?' said Nicky, surprised.

'I hope so,' said Mr Surbans Singh. 'I would not like to eat nothing but chapattis all the year round. Eh, my dear?'

Mrs Mohindar stopped raking and smiled at him.

'I have married a greedy man,' she said.

Mr Surbans Singh looked at the tiny patch he had cut, and then at the vast sweep of the hayfield.

'We have a long way to go,' he said ruefully, and bent to his scything.

From the grey-white hulk of the barns came an erratic clinking of metal. Nicky noticed Gopal looking at her out of the corner of his eye as they walked down the slope.

'What are they up to?' she said nervously.

'Come and see.'

She wouldn't actually go in under the big roof, but the barn was open at both ends and she could see the whole scene. All down one side a rank of bright-coloured engines, gawky with insect-like joints and limbs, stood silent. Other machines and parts of machines littered the floor of the barn, leaving only just enough passageway for the tractors to haul in and out the attachments they needed.

'This farmer liked gadgets,' said Gopal. 'Three combines, two hay-balers, six different tractors, all the latest devices.'

'What are the men doing?' said Nicky, quivering.

Uncle Jagindar was walking about among the engines with a hammer. From time to time he would tap at one, which produced the clinking, and call a man over to him, point and explain.

'Iron and steel are funny stuff,' said Gopal. 'There are lots of different kinds. Some you can work with, and some you can't – it is too hard, or its softening point is too high, or it comes from the forge too brittle. My Uncle Jagindar wants ordinary mild steel, and he's looking for bits he can use; the others are trying to take them off the tractors and attachments.'

'And the things won't go when they're taken to bits?' said Nicky.

'That would suit you?'

'Yes, but it's not as good as smashing them.'

She was quite serious, but Gopal laughed and Uncle Jagindar heard the noise and came out into the sunlight. He was interested in the idea about the bow, but said he didn't think they'd find steel whippy enough, and he didn't think he could temper a rod to that state either. Besides, it would be very dangerous to the bowman if it snapped under tension. Then he shouted to one of the men who brought over an old sickle without a handle which they'd unearthed. Uncle Jagindar sharpened it with a stone and bound sacking tightly round the tang until it was comfortable to hold. Gopal, much to his disgust, was sent up to help Mr Surbans Singh in the hayfield, and Nicky went with him to turn the hay.

It was surprising how much got cut, provided you didn't stop every few minutes to look and see how you were getting on.

4

STEEL ON THE ANVIL

EIGHT days later Nicky went down to the village. She bent her head and ran, with a shudder of disgust, under the double set of power lines that swooped from pylon to pylon across the lane.

'You are afraid that they will fall on you?' asked Uncle Chacha, rolling cat-footed beside her.

'No, it isn't that. But they feel like a . . . like a curse."

'Probably that is why the village people have not come up to disturb us, then.'

'I expect so.'

In fact she could see a whole party of villagers in a field up to their right, almost half a mile away. They were loading a wagon with hay; the wagon was pulled by eight ponies. She pointed.

'They've quite enough fields to work on near the village,' she said, 'without coming up our way.'

'It is curious that they are all working together,' said Uncle Chacha. 'I would have expected them to be cultivating separate patches – that is more the English style. Perhaps somebody has organized them.'

He walked on the verge, keeping close in under the ragged hedge. He was wearing his dull green turban, for extra camouflage. They stopped about fifty yards from the first house, and he tucked himself in behind a bulge of hawthorn.

'If you are in trouble, run this way,' he said. 'But I will not come to help you unless you scream or call.'

'All right,' said Nicky. 'But I'm sure you needn't worry.'

She walked on. It had taken a lot of argument at the council before the Sikhs had agreed that the best way to make contact with the village was for her to go down alone and try to find somebody to talk to. Most of the women had thought it was dangerous, and the men had also felt that it was dishonourable to let a girl take the risk. But the old grandmother had been her ally in the argument, and together they'd won.

The first houses were larger than cottages and looked empty. In front of one of them was a small paddock littered with striped pony-jumps. The next houses were smaller and looked lived in, but there was no sign of life. She rounded the corner into the wider bit of road called The Borough, and there, under the inn-sign of the Five Bells, three men sat on a bench with pewter mugs in their hands.

They looked up as soon as they heard her footfall.

'Good morning,' said Nicky.

The nearest man pushed a battered brown felt hat back over his short-cropped grey hair. His face was brown with sun, and his small grey eyes sharp and suspicious. But he spoke friendly enough.

'And good morning to you, miss,' he said. 'Where're you from, then?'

'I'm staying on the farm up the hill,' said Nicky.

The group tensed. A lean-faced young man with a half-grown beard said, 'Booker's Farm, that'd be?'

'I don't know its name,' said Nicky. 'We just came there and stayed because one of my friends was going to have a baby.'

'How many o' you?' said the hat-wearer.

'About forty.'

They looked at each other.

'That's them,' said a little old man in shirt-sleeves. He spoke with an odd, crowing note.

The others nodded.

'I know what,' said the beard-grower. 'They kep' her prisoner and now she's run away and come to us.'

'No,' said Nicky. 'They helped me get out of London, and so I stayed with them.'

'Bad place, London,' said the man in the hat.

'You aren't one of 'em, though?' crowed the man in shirt-sleeves.

'No,' said Nicky. 'They're called Sikhs.'

'Know what we call 'em?' said the man in the hat. 'We call 'em the Devil's Children.'

'But they aren't like that at all,' said Nicky.

'Leastways they aren't like other folk,' said the man in the hat. 'Not like good Christian folk. You grant me that.'

'They've been very good to me,' said Nicky.

''That's as may be,' said the man in shirt-sleeves. 'We don't want nothing to do with 'em. That's what the Master tells us, and he's right again, too.'

'Is there a smith in the village?' said Nicky.

'Neither there isn't,' said the man in the hat. 'And if there was, he wouldn't care to work for the Devil's Children, would he now?'

The men seemed to become more hostile and suspicious every word they spoke.

'Oh, *we* don't need a smith,' she said. 'But we thought *you* might. For making ploughs and mending spades and things like that. The Sikhs are very good smiths.'

She hoped that was true. The first furnace hadn't blown hot enough, and had to be rebuilt. But the big double bellows had been fashioned from wood and canvas and proved to spout a steady blast of air; and though the first mound of charcoal opened had been poor stuff, and the second not much better, they were all delighted with the product of the new one which had been built on the site of the first.

The three villagers looked at each other, and the one in shirt-sleeves rose to his feet.

'Perhaps I'd best go and fetch him, then,' he said.

'Right you are, Maxie,' said the man in the hat. Maxie scuttled away round the corner.

"And you'd best be up the hayfield, Dunc,' said the man in the hat, 'afore he finds you sitting here swilling of a morning.'

The beard-grower stood up too, but didn't leave.

'Funny thing,' he said. 'I remember my Granny telling me stories about the Queer Folk, and as often as not they

was smiths and iron-workers. Under the hills they used to
live then, she said.'

'That's a fact,' said the man in the hat. 'I remember that
too. Not as I actually thought on it for years and years, but
maybe there's something in it. Maybe they went up to London after.'

'They'll bring you luck, if only you don't cross 'em,' said
the beard-grower eagerly.

'Best have nothing to do with them,' said the man in the
hat.

'But good iron they made,' said the beard-grower. 'Never
wore out, my Granny told me.'

Yes, thought Nicky, it would be easy to believe the Sikhs
were some sort of hobgoblins, if living with them day by
day didn't keep reminding you that they were ordinary
people, bones and veins and muscles and fat. Even she could
only recall in shifting glimpses that other world, before all
these changes happened, where you actually knew about
Sikhs and foreigners without (perhaps) ever having met any.
But these fancies were going to make barter difficult. On
the other hand it meant that the villagers were less likely to
come raiding up to the farm . . .

She was still hesitating what to say next when the little
man, Maxie, came back.

Beside him strode a giant. A man seven foot tall, red-faced
and blue-eyed. He had no waist at all, but a broad leather
belt held shirt and trousers together at the equator of his
prodigious torso. Another strap hung across his shoulder
and from it dangled a naked cutlass. His cheeks were so fat
that separate pads of brick-red flesh bobbled below his eye-
sockets. Nicky noticed that the man in the hat had stood up
when he appeared. The other man, the beard-grower, was
already standing, and it was at him that the giant stared.

' 'Morning, Arthur,' said the man in the hat.

'What you doing down here, Dunc?' said the giant. 'The rest of 'em's up at the hayfield. Them as don't work this summer won't eat this winter.'

'Right you are, Arthur,' said the beard-grower. 'My foot's been playing me up, but it's better now.'

He slipped away, and the blue gaze turned itself on Nicky.

'Who's this, then?' said the giant. His voice was a slow purr, like a well-fed tabby's.

'She says as she lives with the Devil's Children,' explained the man in the hat. 'And she says as they've blacksmiths up there, willing to make and mend for us.'

'So Maxie told me,' said the giant. 'You think we got nothing to do but break good tools, Miss?'

'Oh no,' said Nicky. 'But however careful you are things do get broken, and it isn't going to be so easy to mend them now, or to buy new ones. And I expect there's things you haven't got, like ploughs which you can pull by hand or behind a horse. All the ploughs up at the farm are made for pulling behind those . . . you know . . . tractors.'

As she got the nasty word out the giant took a quick pace forward. She saw a pink thing wheeling towards her but before she had time to duck his open palm, large as a dish, smacked into the side of her head and sent her sprawling. She hadn't even stopped her scraping slide across the dusty tarmac when her shoulders were seized and she was lifted into the air.

She opened her eyes and through the dizziness and tears she saw that the giant was holding her at arm's length, three feet above the ground, so that his face was directly opposite hers. He began to shake her to and fro. As he shook he spoke, in just the same purring voice.

'I'll have no talk (*shake*) like that (*shake*) in my village (*shake*). Not one word of it (*shake*). D'you hear? (*shake*) I'll have no talk (*shake*) like that (*shake*) in my village.'

'Easy, Arthur, easy!' The little man was hanging on to the giant's right elbow. His weight seemed to make no difference at all to the shaking.

'She's only a kid,' crowed the little man, as though he were speaking to the deaf.

The giant stopped shaking and put Nicky down.

'I'd treat my own kids a sight rougher if I heard 'em talking that kind of filth,' he purred.

'But what d'you make of what she was saying before?' said the man in the hat. 'I got a spud-fork needs a good weld. And we'll be crying for hand-ploughs come seed-time.'

'Fetch her your fork then,' said the giant. 'Let's see what sort of a job they do. And then maybe they can show us a ploughshare. You, girl, they'll be wanting something out of us in exchange, won't they, or my name's not Arthur Barnard.'

The vast forefinger pointed suddenly at Nicky as though she'd been trying to cheat him.

'Milk and vegetables and vegetable seed for next year and meat,' she gabbled. 'Not beef. They aren't allowed to eat beef in their religion.'

'Heathen,' purred the giant. 'I'm not having them come among *my* streets, not with fifty ploughs. Fetch her your fork, Tom, and let's see what kind of a job they make of it.'

He turned on his heel and strolled away with four-foot paces. The man and the girl watched him until he was out of earshot.

'Sorry he hit you like that, Miss, but it was your fault for talking nastiness.'

'Yes. Shall I call you Mr Tom?'

'That'll do. Tom Pritchard's me full name.'

'But who is *he?*'

'Arthur Barnard. The Master we call him now. Time was Felpham was full of a different crowd of folk – men went up to London most days, children went away to school, women didn't have enough to do. So *they* ran the village. Then they left, all of a sudden, and only us kind of folk remained. Soon after that a band of ruffians come along, more than twenty of 'em, came here to break and steal and to gobble what food we had. They were that fierce and that rough that most of us were scared to stand up to 'em, and Vicar just shut himself in the Church and prayed, but Arthur Barnard – cowman he used to be, up at Ironside's – he drove 'em out. Took that sword he wears out of the old admiral's cottage and drove 'em out. Pretty nigh on single-handed he did it. Since then what he says goes, like as you've seen. You come with me, miss, and we'll find that fork.'

He limped away to his council house up beyond the church. The fork had been broken just above where the handle joined the tines. One long strip of iron still ran up the front of the wood, but the wood itself was snapped and the strip of iron behind had rusted right through.

Uncle Chacha turned the tool over discontentedly in the shelter of the hedge and listened to Nicky's story.

'I do not know,' he said. 'Perhaps Jagindar can mend it, but it does not look easy. This is not my trade; I am a checker in a warehouse, not a blacksmith. Does your head hurt where the man hit you?'

'I'm getting used to being hit,' said Nicky, fingering the bruised bone. 'He wasn't quite so quick as you are, but his hand was much heavier.'

Uncle Chacha nodded, put the fork over his shoulder and started on the trudge up the lane. After a while he said, 'This man sounds interesting. A smaller fighter can sometimes defeat a bigger one because he is quicker, but a man who is very big and quite quick will usually win.'

'If you were a checker in a warehouse,' said Nicky, 'how do you know so much about fighting, and why are you so good at it?'

'I am very quick,' said Uncle Chacha, 'because all my life I have played squash. I am quite good – I have played in the national championships, though I did not get very far. I have also learnt some judo, because I was not very popular at the warehouse when I first went there. The other men were racially intolerant, and I wished to be able to defend myself. A Sikh should know how to fight.'

'But swords and things,' said Nicky.

'Oh, we will have to see.'

They got the forge going two days later. Nicky stood in the doorway of the shed, where the stolid sun beat brilliant against the brick, and watched a pair of uncles pumping rhythmically at the bellows-bar in the dusky interior. The pulses of air roared with a deep, hungry note as they drove through the glowing charcoal, turning it from dull red to orange and from orange to searing yellow. Uncle Jagindar stood in the orange cone of light from the furnace door, shading his eyes as he gazed against the glare. He was stripped to the waist and the weird light cast blue shadows between the ridges of his muscles. At last he grunted and nodded, and Mr Gurchuran Singh picked up a pair of pincers and lifted a short bar of white-hot metal from the furnace. When it was steady on the anvil Uncle Jagindar smote steadily at it with a four-pound hammer. The brightness died out of it as though the blows were killing the light; the crash of each blow rang so sharp, and the next crash followed it so quickly, that Nicky's head began to ring with the racket and she put her hands to her ears. Kewal took her by the elbow and led her away.

'Is it all right?' he said. His anxiety seemed to make his squint worse than ever.

'Oh yes,' said Nicky. 'Only it's so *noisy*. What are they making?'

'Just a practice piece, a small sword for one of the children. It may not be very good because Jagindar is not sure of the quality of the steel he is using. Steel is a mixture of iron and carbon in exact quantities, and the hot charcoal adds more carbon to the iron, so you achieve steel of a different temper. In primitive conditions like this it is all a matter of judgement, so the first few things he makes will probably be flawed or brittle.'

Nicky looked down the slope to where two extraordinary figures were prancing on the unmown lawn behind the farmhouse. Their padded necks and shoulders made them look heavy and gawky, but they skipped around each other like hares in March, taking vicious swipes at the padding with short curved staves. Few of the swipes reached their target because the figures ducked and backed so agilely, or took the blow cunningly on the little round leather shields which Uncle Chacha had cut from old trunks in the farmhouse attic. Suddenly Nicky realized that the six-yard folds of fine linen from which the Sikhs contrived their turbans would be almost as useful in battle as a steel helmet. The fencing practice stopped, and Uncle Chacha and Mr Harbans Singh leaned on their staves and discussed what they had learnt.

'Yes,' said Nicky, 'I suppose a brittle sword wouldn't last long with that amount of bashing. But I thought proper fencers prodded at each other with the points of their swords, instead of swiping like that.'

'It is a different type of sword,' said Kewal. 'We Sikhs have always used the tulwar, which you call a sabre. The curve of the blade helps the cutting edge to slice through whatever you strike at. You Europeans invented the duelling sword, using the point to pierce your enemy before he could reach you, but even European cavalry has always used the sabre because the horse carries a man to close quarters where the cutting edge is handier than the point.'

'I hope he doesn't make Mr Tom's fork brittle,' said Nicky. 'Let's go and help in the hayfield.'

Kewal made a face, but walked up the path beside her. Nicky was learning all sorts of surprising differences between the Sikhs, who had at first seemed so like each other. Kewal, for instance, was quick and clever, but lazy and vain; most days he seemed to have some reason to wear his smartest clothes, and the clothes then became a reason for not doing any hard or dirty work – though he was usually on the fringe of any working party, criticizing and giving advice. If Nicky had suggested going up to the wood to help in the endless job of carting charcoal down to the forge, he'd have found a reason for doing something else. The black and brittle treasure from the opened mounds filled all the air around with a fine and filthy dust. That was work too dirty for Kewal.

Suddenly Nicky laughed aloud. *She* was going up to the hayfield as an excuse for not taking her turn at the flour-milling, which she thought the dreariest job on the whole farm : you pounded and rubbed and sieved for an hour, and finished with two cupfuls. Kewal looked to see if he could share the joke, but she shook her head.

The toy sword was given to Kaka and he swaggered about with it stuck into his straining belt, looking just like a mini-

ature version of the giant down in the village. Uncle Jagindar was pleased with it, because it didn't snap when you bent
it or banged the anvil with it, and the edge came up killing
sharp. He practised all next day at the forge and on the third
day he mended Mr Tom's fork, welding a new length of
steel up the back. The Rissaldar shaped a new handle, and
the finished job looked almost as good as a fork from a shop.
Nicky was ready to take it down at once, but Gopal said,
'No, listen!'

The bells were going in the church tower, tumbling
sweetly through their changes. It must be Sunday. The Sikhs
didn't keep Sunday or any other day as special; instead they
had long prayers and readings from their holy book morning and evening. Yes, it would be a mistake to go down on a
Sunday, another sign of how different the two communities
were.

She found Mr Tom at his house on Monday morning. He
fingered the weld and the new handle with hands so harsh
that you could hear his skin scrape across the surface.

'Clean and sturdy, I'd say,' he said. 'We'll show the
Master. He's in court, Mondays.'

They found the giant in what had been a classroom in the
school. Mr Tom led Nicky quietly in and pointed to a bench
where she could sit. Twenty other villagers were there,
crammed behind child-sized desks; the giant sat up on the
dais, also cramped, though his desk had been made for a
grown man. Maxie sat at a table below the dais, scribbling
in a ledger. A dark, angry-looking woman stood in front of
the desk complaining about something. When she stopped
she sat down. The giant looked at the room in silence for a
full minute.

Then he nodded to Maxie, who had stopped writing.
Maxie leapt to his feet and crowed like a cock.

'Now hear this!' were the words he crowed. The giant purred into the silence.

'Mrs Sallow,' he said, 'has brought a complaint against her neighbour Mr Goddard, saying that his dog spoils her flower-beds by burying bones in 'em. There are three points to this case. Firstly, it is the nature of a dog to bury its bones where it feels like, and you can't change that. Secondly, flower beds aren't of no account in Felpham no more – it's vegetables we'll be needing, beans and such, to see us through the coming winter. Thirdly, which falls into two parts, a man must have a good dog, and if that dog goes digging up the neighbour's flower beds the neighbour has to put up with it though it would be different, like I said, if it was vegetables. And moreover it is the use and custom of Felpham that a woman is subservient to a man, and when it comes to a complaint, other things being equal, the man shall have the best of it. Case dismissed.'

'Case dismissed,' crowed Maxie and began to scribble again in his ledger.

The dark woman, looking angrier than ever, bustled out of the classroom.

'That's the last case, eh, Maxie?' said the giant.

'Yessir.'

Mr Tom stood up.

'The girl's brought my spud-fork back from the Devil's Children,' he said. 'Seems like a good mend to me.'

'Let's have a squint at it,' said the giant.

Tom took the fork up to the dais and the giant rose from his desk. First he waggled the tool to and fro in his huge hands, then he peered at the actual join, then he took the tines in one hand and the handle in the other, put his knee to the join and heaved.

'Oi!' cried Mr Tom. 'Don't you go busting of it, Arthur!'

The giant stopped heaving and gazed at Mr Tom from under reddish eyebrows. Mr Tom looked away, and the giant resumed heaving. Nicky could see the squares of his check shirt change shape where they crossed his shoulders as the ox-like muscles bulged with the effort. The classroom was silent as a funeral. Suddenly there came a crack and a twang, and the fork changed shape.

The giant straightened and held it up. He had snapped the wooden handle clean in two, and one of the steel supports had broken with it, but the other had held. It was the piece Uncle Jagindar had mended which had stayed unbroken.

'Now hear this,' purred the giant panting slightly with the aftermath of that great spasm of strength.

'Now hear this!' crowed Maxie.

'We'll be needing a fair whack of honest tools,' said the giant. 'Some will want mending, and some we haven't got. You all know how the Devil's Children have settled in up at Booker's, and how near we came to raiding up there and driving 'em out, wires or no bad wires. Now it turns out that they've blacksmiths among them, as will make and mend ironwork for us, and do an honest job at it. So I say this: if a man wants a piece of iron mended, or made, he'll come to me and tell me what he wants, and I'll fix a fair price for him with this girl here, as lives with the Devil's Children. If you want a job done, you must pay a fair price. But I won't fix a price which the village nor the man can't spare, I promise you that. It'll be a bag of carrots, maybe, for a mended spade, and a lamb or two for a new plough. And I hereby appoint Tom Pritchard my deputy to handle this trade, seeing as I broke your fork, Tom, though I'll oversee it myself till we've got it running smoothly. But if I find one of you, or any other man or woman in Felpham, dealing with the Devil's Children direct, other than through me or Tom Pritchard and this girl here, I'll skin 'em alive, I promise you that. We have to trade with 'em, but they're heathen, outlandish heathen, and apart from trade we don't want to see nor hide nor hair of 'em. I've heard some of you talking fancy about them, saying as they're the Queer Folk and suchlike rubbish. I don't want to hear no more of that. They're mortal flesh, like you and me. But they're heathen foreigners besides, and it is the use and custom of Felpham to have nothing to do with 'em. Now, such of you as've got metal to make and mend, you're to bring it to the Borough, or drawings of what you want. Maxie, you can cry the news through the village. Court adjourned.'

'Court adjourned,' crowed Maxie and whisked out of the room like a blown leaf. Tom went ruefully up to the dais to collect his ruined fork; Nicky saw that he was too afraid of the giant to complain. She sat where she was while the room cleared; all the time the giant stared at the wall above the door, as though he could see through it.

When the last of the villagers had gone he yawned, scratched the back of his head, stood up, settled his cutlass-strap over his shoulder, covered it with an orange cloak which he pinned in place with a big brooch, clapped a broad hat with a plume in it on to his head and strode towards the door. Nicky saw that he was wearing boots now, and that the cloak had once been a curtain. The room boomed at every footfall. He stopped suddenly, as though he'd only just noticed her.

'What are you waiting for, girl?' he said.

'I wanted to ask you how we're going to fix a proper price for the work if you won't meet any of the Sikhs.'

'The Devil's Children,' he said.

'They aren't like that at all,' said Nicky. 'They're proud,

and they wear funny clothes, and they talk a lot, but when you get to know them they're really like anybody else. Just ordinary.'

'None of my folk's going to get to know the Devil's Children,' said the giant without looking at her. 'But I give you my honour I'll strike a fair price. Think, girl, it's in my interest till we can find a smith of our own; there's a heap of metalwork to be done before winter if we're to come through it short of starving. I don't want your people trading over to Aston, nor Fadlingfield, because they think we've cheated 'em here. Now you run along. This afternoon I'll send a barrow of stuff up as far as the bad wires; you can fetch it back, mended, this day week. We're vicious short on scythes, too, so you can get your friends to forge us half-a-dozen new 'uns – we'll shape the handles.'

'All right,' said Nicky and turned to go.

'Come back, girl,' said the giant. 'I've more to say. You heard what I told my people about having nothing to do with the Devil's Children. You tell your friends the same. If I see one of those brown skins down this side of the bad wires I'll tear him apart, man, woman or child. Joint by joint I'll tear him.'

There was no point in arguing, so Nicky walked out into the mid-morning glare and ran down the street, left through the Borough and up the lane to where Kewal was waiting for her in the shadow of the hedge. (Now that the job was known to be safe he had volunteered for it because it was also known to be easy.) He was almost as interested by the description of the court as Uncle Chacha had been by the first meeting with the giant.

'Yes,' he said. 'He is becoming a feudal baron, and he is setting about it the right way. It would be curious to know whether he has thought it out or whether his behaviour is instinctive. The first step is to make all the villagers obey him, and this he must do partly by frequent demonstrations of his physical strength – that was why he broke the fork – and partly by laying down strict rules which they *can* obey. And at the same time he must channel all the business

of the village through his own hands. Now a man who wants a fork mended or a scythe made must come to him, and if that man is out of favour with him then the work will not be done. So our forge is another source of power for him.'

'He protects them too, don't forget,' said Nicky. 'And I thought they seemed to like being bullied like that, in a funny way.'

'Oh yes, of course. Most people prefer to have their think-

ing done for them. Democracy is not a natural growth, it is a
weary responsibility. You have to be sterling fellows, such
as we Sikhs are, to make it work.'

That afternoon two barrow-loads of broken implements
waited where the power-lines crossed the lane. Uncle Jagindar and his assistants toiled in the roaring and clanging
smithy as long as there was light. By Friday the work was
done.

The giant scrutinized tool after tool in the Borough before handing them back to their owners, but as far as Nicky
could tell from the blue unwinking eyes and the blubbery
cheeks he was satisfied. She explained about the pieces
which Uncle Jagindar had said were past mending, and he
nodded. Half an hour later she was herding two fat lambs
up the lane, while a disgruntled Kewal toiled behind her
shoving a barrow piled high with vegetables.

5

LOST BOY

THE sheep meant more work – hurdles to be woven from thin-sliced strips of chestnut, posts to be rammed into the ground to hold the hurdles steady in sheep-proof fences round an area where the hay had been cut. Then the fences had to be moved every two days to allow the flock to get at fresh grass. And men had to sleep out at the sheep-fold all night to scare away wild dogs and foxes The flock rose to about thirty animals by the end of August, so steadily did the smithy work; in fact Nicky and Kewal decided that the giant must be extending his empire by trading in metalwork with villages on the far side of Felpham, so many broken tools did he seem to find, so many orders for scythes and ploughshares and horse-harness were left each week with the barrows.

Nicky asked him one day if he could pay for the next big load with a horse, but he stared at her angrily and shook his head.

'I hear as they're carrying swords now,' he purred suspiciously; the huge hand crept to the pommel of his cutlass.

'Yes,' said Nicky. 'It's part of their religion. They were soldiers ages ago, and they've always carried swords. My friends used to wear a little toy sword before ... before ... you know; now they've made themselves proper ones again, in case they have to fight somebody.'

'And now they're wanting horses too,' said the giant. Suddenly Nicky saw what was worrying him.

'But they don't want horses for fighting on,' she said.

'They don't want to fight anybody. They'd like horses for ploughing and pulling carts and so on.'

'That's as may be,' said the giant. 'But I'm not sparing horses. I've given you a fair price for the work so far, haven't I?'

'Oh yes,' said Nicky and looked at a crate of baffled hens which was balanced across one of the barrows. 'The Sikhs are very pleased.'

'And so they ought to be,' said the giant. 'Well, if they're making swords for themselves, they can make 'em for me, too.'

'I'll ask,' said Nicky doubtfully.

'You do that,' said the giant, and sauntered down the hill. He moved nowadays with a slow and lordly gait which seemed to imply that all the wide landscape belonged to him, and every creature in it.

But Uncle Jagindar refused to make weapons for anybody except his own people, and the Sikh council (though they argued the question round for twenty minutes) all agreed with him. When he heard the news the giant became surlier than ever with Nicky, and the villagers copied him. Partly, Nicky decided, this was because they just did whatever *he* did out of sheer awe of him; but it was also partly because of the way they had built up a whole network of myths and imaginings around the Sikhs. One or two things that Maxie said, or Mr Tom when he was talking over smithwork to be done, showed that their heads were full of crazy notions. They stopped looking her in the face when they spoke to her, as though they were afraid of some power that might rest in her eye. Also, if there were children in The Borough when she came past, mothers' voices would yell a warning and little legs would scuttle for doorways. Once Nicky even saw a soapy arm reach through a window and grab a baby by the leg from where it was sleeping in a sort of wooden pram.

The giant still looked her straight in the eye, and raged in his purring voice if he heard anyone suggest or hint that the Devil's Children were other than human flesh, but the scary whisperings went on behind his back. Nicky first realized how strong these dotty beliefs had become when she found the lost boy.

August had been a furiously busy month. The smithy furnace still roared all day, eating charcoal by the sackful. Ajeet and Nicky were officially in charge of the chickens, but that didn't excuse them from any other work that needed doing – looking after babies, or chasing escaped sheep, or dreary milling, or binding and stooking the untidy sheaves as the first wheat was reaped, and there were six scythes now to do the reaping. And then, a few days later, the dried sheaves were carried down to the lane and spread about for threshing; and that was woman's work, though after twenty minutes' drubbing at the gold mass with the clumsy threshing-flail your neck and shoulders ached with sharp pain and your hands were all blisters.

But even threshing was better than ploughing, which Mr Surbans Singh insisted on making an experimental start on as soon as the sheaves were off the stubble.

'We are learning new sums,' whispered Ajeet. 'Four children equal one horse.'

Nicky only grunted. She was trudging with six-inch steps through the shin-scratching stalks, leaning her weight right forward against the rope that led over the pad on her shoulder and back to the plough-frame. Ajeet trudged beside her with another rope, and Gopal and his cousin Harpit just ahead; behind her Mr Surbans Singh wrestled with the bucking plough-handles as the blade surged in jolts and rushes through roots and flinty earth. It was very slow, very tiring, and turned only a wiggling, shallow furrow. When at last Mr Surbans Singh called halt, all four children sank groaning to the bristly stubble and watched while Mr Surbans Singh and Uncle Jagindar and Mr Wazir Singh (who had once been a farmer) scuffed at the turned earth with their feet, bent to trickle it through their fingers, and discussed the tilt and angle of the blade.

'Not bad,' said Mr Surbans Singh at last. 'We cannot plough all these acres. The next thing is to take sharp poles and search for the best patches of earth.'

'You can run away and play now, children,' said Mr Wazir Singh, who was one of those people who always manage to talk to children as though they are small and stupid and anything they do, even when they've been helping for all they're worth, was of no interest or importance.

'Thank you, Nicky,' said Mr Surbans Singh with his brilliant smile. She could see where broad streams of sweat had runnelled through the dust on his face, and realized that he must have been toiling twice as hard as any of them.

'Thank you, Ajeet and Gopal and Harpit,' he went on. 'Ask your Aunt Mohindar to give you each an apple.'

The apples in the artist's cottage garden weren't ready for eating yet, but the village had paid for some of the last lot of work with a sack of James Grieves. The children sat on the wall round the well and bit into the white flesh, so juicy that there was no way of stopping the sweet liquid flowing down the outside of their chins in wasteful dribbles. Nicky looked over the wide gold landscape, where the swifts hurtled and wheeled above wheat that would never be harvested, and felt the wanderlust on her. Suddenly the close community, busy with its ceaseless effort for survival, seemed stifling.

Usually she would have gone for rest and calm to sit by the old lady's cart under the wych-elm, and watched the babies playing. Even when Ajeet came to translate, she and the old lady did not speak much, though sometimes the old lady would tell her of extraordinary things she had seen and done in that other life before she came to England – not really as though she was trying to entertain Nicky, more to teach her, to instruct, to pass on precious knowledge. And when they didn't speak, it was still soothing to be near her, in a way that Nicky couldn't explain; she guessed that the old lady felt the same, but there was no way of asking.

But today the old lady had one of her little illnesses and had stayed in bed, not wanting to see anybody except her daughters, and then only to complain to them about something. So now Nicky longed to be out of earshot of the clang of the forge and the thud of the flails, away from the pricking and clotting dust which all this hard work stirred into the air, somewhere else.

'I'm going for a walk,' she said as she threw her core away.

Harpit groaned. Gopal sighed.

'So I shall have to come with you,' he said, 'to slaughter your enemies.'

He patted the three-quarter-size sword that swung against his hip. He was very proud of it because Uncle Jagindar said it was the best blade he'd made. One corner of the forge held a pile of snapped blades which hadn't stood up to the cruel testing the smiths gave them. ('What use is a sword,' Uncle Chacha had asked, 'if you strike with it once and then there is nothing left in your hand but the hilt?') Gopal joined the adults for fencing-practice these days.

Now he patted his sword like a warrior and stood up.

'I'm afraid I haven't got any enemies for you,' said Nicky as she stood too.

'Not even the bad baron?' said Harpit. That was what the children called the giant down in the village. It was funny to think that Nicky was the only one who'd ever seen him.

'No, he's not my enemy,' said Nicky. 'He's all right – in fact he's a hero, sort of.'

'I must tell my mother where we're going,' whispered Ajeet.

'I will tell her,' said Harpit, 'and that means I need not come on this idiot expedition. Where are you going, Nicky?'

'Up to the Common.'

Despite Gopal's sword, Nicky was the one who led the way down the curving line of elms and oaks that had been allowed to stay on the boundary between one farm and the next; the ripe barley brushed against their left shoulders; they dipped into the place where the line of trees became a farm track, whose slope took them down to join a magical and haunted lane, untarred, running nearly fifteen feet below the level of the surrounding fields. The hedge trees at the top of the banks on either side met far above their heads, so that the children walked in a cool green silence and looked up into the caverns where the earth had been washed away from between blanched tree-roots. In that convenient dark the animals of the night laired. It was a street of foxes.

Then, too soon, they were out into the broad evening sun and turning left up the grassy track to the Common. Swayne's farm, deserted now, stood silent on the corner – mainly a long wall of windowless brick, with gates opening into yards where cattle had once mooched and scuffled. Gopal, driven by some impulse to assert himself against the brooding stillness, drew the grey curved blade from his belt and lunged at imaginary foes; with each lunge he gave a grunting cry. The echo bounced off the brick wall on the far side of the farmyard, and died into stillness.

'Please stop it,' said Ajeet. Gopal sheathed his sword, grinning.

The echo continued. It said 'Help!'

Nicky climbed the gate into the farmyard. The dry litter rustled under her feet.

'Where are you?' she called.

'Here,' said the faint voice. 'Help! I'm stuck!'

They found him in the loft over a cow-byre. A ladder lay on the floor of the byre, and in the square black hole in the ceiling a wan face floated. Nicky and Gopal lifted the fallen ladder back into place.

'I can't climb down,' said the face. 'I've hurt my foot.' It began to sob.

'I'll come up and help you,' said Gopal. 'Don't worry. It's all right.'

'Not you!' wailed the face. 'I've got a brick. I'll hit you!'

Gopal took his hand off the rung and shrugged.

Nicky climbed slowly up the ladder. The face shifted in the square, and in the dimness behind she saw an arm move upwards. She stopped climbing.

'It's quite all right,' she said. 'I won't hurt you. My name's Nicky Gore. What's yours?'

'Shan't tell you.'

The arm with the brick wavered uncertainly. Nicky flinched.

'Look,' she said, 'if I'd got magic your brick wouldn't hurt me, but if I haven't got magic then you'd be hurting somebody just like yourself, somebody who's trying to help you.'

'What about him?' said the boy, still panting with sobs.

'He wants to help you too. His name's Gopal. He's my

friend. And the other one's Ajeet — she tells wonderful stories.'

'Tell 'em to go away.'

Nicky looked over her shoulder. Ajeet was already floating out like a shadow. Gopal shrugged again, tested the bottom of the ladder and went to the door.

'Be careful,' he said. 'I *think* it's steady, but not if you start fighting on it.'

Nicky managed a sort of laugh as she climbed into the darkness.

'How long have you been here?' she said.

'I have been here all day. I was looking for treasure. There's a heap of treasure buried up on the Common, folk say, but when I come to the farm I thought the farm folk might have found some, so I started looking here, and then I knocked the ladder down, and then I trod on a bit o' glass and it come clean through my foot . . .'

He was about eight, very dirty, the dirt on his face all streaked with blubbering.

'Wriggle it round over the hole,' said Nicky, 'and I'll have a look.'

He did so, with slow care; his groans sounded like acting, but the foot really did look horrid; the worn plimsoll was covered with dried blood and the foot seemed to bulge unnaturally inside the canvas. The laces were taut and too knotted to undo, so Nicky drew her hunting-knife (which Uncle Chacha had honed for her to a desperate sharpness) and sliced them delicately through. The boy cried aloud as the pressure altered, then sat sobbing. Nicky realized that she'd probably done the wrong thing. They must get him to an adult as soon as possible.

'Look,' she said, 'if I go down the ladder the wrong way round, then you can get yourself further over the hole, and

I'll come back up until you're sitting on my shoulders. Then I can give you a piggy-back down.'

The boy nodded dully. Nicky stepped on to the ladder and went down until her head was below floor-level. There she turned so that her heels were on the rungs.

'Now,' she said, 'see if you can wriggle your bottom along until your good leg is right over this side. A bit further. Now I'm coming up a rung. I'll hold your leg so that it doesn't bang anything.'

'It hurts frightful when I drop it,' groaned the boy.

'All right, I'll hold it up. Now you take hold of the ladder, lean forward against my head, and see if you can lift your bottom across so that you're sitting on the rung. Well done! Now let yourself slide down on to my shoulders; hold on to my forehead. Higher, you're covering my eyes. Hold tight. Down we go!'

The ladder creaked beneath the double weight. Nicky moved one heel carefully to the next rung, bending her knee out steadily so as to lower the two of them without a jolt. The wounded foot came through the opening with an inch to spare. Each rung seemed to take ages, as the thigh-muscles above her bending knee were stretched to aching iron. She'd done five and was resting for the next when the grip on her forehead suddenly gave way.

'Hold tight!' she cried and flung up her hand from the ladder to catch the slipping arm.

'Are you all right?' she said.

There was no answer. The boy's weight was now quite limp. Fresh blood was seeping, bright scarlet, through the crackled dark rind of the blood which had dried on his shoe before. Gopal, who must have been watching through the doorway, ran in and held the bottom of the ladder. She came down the last few rungs in one rush, trying to hold the boy

from falling by forcing the back of her head into his stomach to slide him down the rungs. The top of the ladder bounced and rattled in the trap-door, but stayed put.

'I've got his shoulders,' said Gopal. 'We've found something to carry him on outside. Can you manage?'

Nicky staggered out into the sunlight and saw Ajeet spreading hay on to a hurdle.

'This end,' said Gopal. 'Turn your back to it. Now get down as low as you can and I'll lift him off.'

Nicky crouched, then sat; she twisted to ease the wounded leg on to the hay, and at last stood, shuddering with the long effort and feeling such sudden lightness that a breeze could have blown her away.

'Well done, Nicky,' said Gopal. 'Lift his leg, Ajeet, while I put more hay under it. If we get it higher than the body it might bleed less badly. And then we will need to lash it into place, so that it does not flop about while we are carrying him. A rope or a strap.'

'No,' said Ajeet, 'something softer. What about your puggri?'

'It is such a nuisance to do up again,' said Gopal ruefully, but he began to unwind the long folds of his turban. His black hair fell over his shoulders, like a girl's, but he twisted it up with a few practised flicks and pinned it into place with the square wooden comb. The cloth was long enough to go three times round the hurdle, lashing the leg comfortably firm. The child muttered and stirred, but did not wake. His face looked a nasty yellowy-grey beneath the tear-streaked dirt.

'Where shall we take him?' said Nicky.

'Up to the farm,' said Gopal.

'He won't like that,' said Nicky. 'Nor will the villagers. They'll think we've stolen his soul away, or something.'

'Never mind,' said Gopal. 'First, we don't know which house, or even which village, to take him to. Second, he must have proper medical attention, and he won't get *that* in the village.'

'All right,' said Nicky.

Gopal took the front of the hurdle, Nicky and Ajeet the two back corners. The first stretch, along the deep lane, was manageable, but after that it became harder even than ploughing, and they had to rest every fifty yards. They were battling up through the barley-field when a voice hissed at them from the trees. They stopped and looked into the shadow, too tired to be frightened.

It was the Rissaldar, statuesque with his long bow, waiting for a rabbit or a pheasant. Obviously he was cross that they had spoiled his hunting, but after a question or two in Punjabi, answered by Gopal, he stepped out from his cover, handed the bow to Nicky, and took the girl's end of the hurdle. For the rest of the journey the children worked shift and shift on the front corners.

The communal supper was being carried out of the artist's cottage when they at last settled the hurdle wearily across the well-head. The usual cackle of argument rose as the women gathered round the wounded boy, while the steam from the big bowls of curry rose pungent through the evening air, but Cousin Punam shushed the cooks away and had the hurdle carried into one of the sheds beside the farmyard.

'We will take the sock and shoe off while he's still fainted,' she said, snipping busily with a pair of nail-scissors. 'Then he will never know how much it hurts, eh? I did not think, when I was doing my training, that so soon I would have to be a qualified doctor. A little boiled water, a little disinfectant, cotton wool . . . Ai, but that's a nasty cut! Pull very gently at this bit of sock, Nicky, while I cut here. Ah, how dirty! That's it, good – throw it straight on the fire. And don't come back for five minutes, Nicky, because now I must do something you will not like.'

It was still more than an hour till nightfall. The last gold of sunset lay slant across the fields and in it the swifts still wheeled, hundreds of feet up, too high for her to hear their bloodless screaming. It was going to be another blazing day tomorrow, just right for the dreary toil of reaping and threshing. She leaned against the cottage wall and looked down at the square brick tower of the church, warm in that warm light. What next? The boy would be in trouble in the village if they learnt he had crossed the bad wires; if the Sikhs simply put him on the hurdle and carried him down to the Borough, they could expect more suspicion than gratitude – and Cousin Punam *had* been going to do something 'wrong' to him . . . Nicky would have to remind her to tie the wound up with a clean rag, and not anything out of her bag . . .

Cousin Punam had finished, but was talking to someone. Nicky heard the words '. . . tetanus injection . . .' before she called out to ask whether she could come in. Neena was sponging the grime off the sleeping face.

'When will he wake up?' said Nicky.

'Quite soon, perhaps,' said Cousin Punam.

'It sounds awful,' said Nicky, 'but he'll be terrified if he sees you. Let me wait, and I'll find out where he lives. Then we can take him back.'

Cousin Punam sighed and shrugged, just as Gopal had done down at Swayne's.

'Have you had your supper, Nicky?' said Neena.

'Not yet.'

'I'll send you some.'

'Thank you,' said Nicky. 'And thank you, Punam, for ...
everything.'

She stumbled over the words, half conscious that she was
speaking for the boy and his mother and the whole village
words that they would never learn to say. The women left.
Ajeet came back with a chapatti – the heavy, scone-like
bread which the Sikhs made – and mutton curry. Nicky was
just learning to like the taste now that the Sikhs were beginning to run out of curry-powder.

Perhaps it was the smell of food which woke the boy,
because he tried to sit up when Ajeet was hardly out of the
stall. Nicky rose from the floor, her mouth crammed with
bread and curry.

'Don't try to move,' she mumbled. 'How does your leg
feel?'

He looked at it as though he'd forgotten how it hurt, then
at her, then, wide-eyed, round the dim unfamiliar stall.

'Where's the rest of them?' he whispered.

'Having their supper. You're all right. We'll look after
you.'

'I'm not telling you my name,' he whispered fiercely.
'My mum says don't tell 'em your name if they catch you,
and they've got no power on you, 'cause they don't know
what to call you in their spells.'

'If you'll tell me where you live, we'll carry you home as
soon as it's dark.'

'Oh,' he said with a note of surprise.

'I thought we could say you'd been looking for birds'
nests in the hedge below the bad wires, and one of us heard
you calling and found you'd hurt your foot and brought you
up here. Then nobody'd know you'd crossed the wires.'

'Much too late for birds' nests,' he said. 'Where you come
from, if you don't know that?'

'London,' said Nicky. 'Well, you think of something you might have been looking for at this time of year.'

"Too early for crabs or nuts,' said the boy. 'Tell you what: I could have been looking for a rabbit-run to put a snare in.'

'That'll do,' said Nicky, thinking that she ought to tell the Rissaldar about rabbit snares. 'Do you live in the village or outside it?'

'Right agin the edge,' he said. 'You can cut across to our back garden through Mr Banstead's paddock.'

'Good,' said Nicky. 'We won't go till it's nearly dark. I'm afraid your mother will be worrying for you.'

'That she will,' said the boy.

'Are you hungry?'

Suspicion tightened the lines of his face again.

'I'm not eating the Queer Folk's food,' he muttered.

'I could bring you water from the well,' Nicky suggested. 'That was here before us. And there's a bag of apples which came up from the village only yesterday morning.'

He thought for a few seconds, hunger and terror fighting.

'All right,' he said at last.

After supper they lifted him gently back on to his hurdle and four of the Uncles carried him down the lane. He stared at his bearers in mute fear until, between step and step, he fell deep asleep. Nicky had to shake him awake at the edge of the village so that he could tell them their way through the dusk.

It was the last cottage in the lane to Halling Down. The Uncles lowered the hurdle on to the dewy grass and stole off into the darkness by the paddock hedge. A dog yelped in the cottage next door as Nicky pushed the sagging gate open. A man's voice shouted at the dog. The door at the end of the path opened, sending faint gold across a cabbage-patch. A woman stood in the rectangle of light. Nicky walked up the path.

'That you, Mike?' called the woman.

The boy cried faintly to her from his hurdle.

'I found him hurt,' said Nicky, 'so we bandaged him up and brought him home.'

The woman picked up her long skirts and rushed down the path. It was the same Mrs Sallow who'd been complaining in court about her neighbour's dog. When Nicky got back to the paddock she was kneeling by the stretcher with her arm under the boy's shoulders.

'His foot's very bad,' said Nicky. 'I think I could manage one end if you do the other.'

Mrs Sallow stood up and looked despairingly round. Obviously her feud with the dog-owner meant she could expect no help from there, and she had no neighbour on the other side.

'All right,' she said. 'But mind you, I owe you nothing.'

'Of course not,' said Nicky.

The boy and the hurdle weighed like death. The boy groaned as they tilted through the gateway. The woman said nothing. Nicky lowered her end on the path outside the door.

'I'll cope from here,' said the woman. She knelt by the hurdle and pulled the boy to her. Then with a painful effort she staggered to her feet. Nicky held the door open for her.

'You keep out,' said the woman.

'I never told 'em my name, Mum,' said the boy.

'Good lad,' said the woman.

'But, Mum . . .' said the boy.

'Tell me later,' she said, and kicked the door shut with her heel.

Nicky had dragged the hurdle down the path and joined

the Uncles by the hedge when the cottage door opened again. Mrs Sallow stood in the doorway, hands on her hips, head thrown back.

'You people,' she called. 'I give you my thanks for what you have done for my boy.'

The door shut as the neighbour's dog exploded into an ecstasy of yelping.

'What was the significance of that?' said Mr Surbans Singh.

'It's unlucky to take help from fairies,' explained Nicky, 'if you don't thank them. All the stories say so. Goodness I'm tired.'

'In that case,' said Mr Surbans Singh, 'it is most fortunate that we happen to have a magic hurdle here, with four demons to carry it.'

So Nicky rode home through the dark while the Uncles made low-voiced jokes about their supernatural powers. It was almost a month before she saw Mike Sallow again.

6

THIEVES' HARVEST

THEY had been ploughing all day, with four ploughs going and every man and woman, as well as all the older children, taking turns at the heavy chore. Between turns they worked at the two strips which were wanted for autumn sowing, breaking down the clods with hoes and dragging the harrow to and fro to produce a fine tilth. The thin strips of turned earth looked pitiful amid the rolling steppes of stubble and unmown wheat. The strips were scattered apparently at random over the farm, wherever prodding with sticks had shown the soil to be deepest or least flinty, or where there seemed some promise of shelter from the winds. There'd been no rain for a week, so the soil was light and workable, which was why the whole community was slaving at it to-day. On other days logging parties had been up in the woods, getting in fuel for the winter. And twice a raiding party had set off at dusk, trekked the twenty miles to Reading through the safe night, stayed in the empty city all day, and trekked back laden with stores and blocks of the most precious stuff in all England, salt.

But today had been stolid ploughing. Resting between her turns, Nicky had been vaguely conscious that something was happening down in the village. The bells rang for a minute, not their proper changes, and then stopped. Shouts drifted up against the breeze, but so faint and far that she didn't piece them together into a coherent sequence or even realize that they were more and louder than they might have been.

About six it was time to go and get the hens in by scatter-ing corn in their coops. If you left it later than that they tried to roost out in the shrubs of the farmhouse garden. She was helping Ajeet search the tattered lavender-bushes for hidden nests when she saw, down the lane and out of the corner of her eye, a furtive movement – somebody ducking into the crook of the bank to avoid being seen. Kewal, she thought, out checking the rabbit snares to escape his share of ploughing. But Kewal had been up in the field, lugging at the ropes as steadily as anyone (it was really only that he didn't like *starting* jobs) and besides, hadn't the shape in the lane had fair hair? And wasn't there something awkward about the way it had moved?

Inquisitive, she slid down the bank and stole along the lane. They all went bare-footed as often as possible now, because shoes were wearing out and making new ones was a job for winter evenings. No Council workmen had been along the lanes of England that summer, keeping the verges trim, so you could bury yourself deep in the rank grasses. Mike, peering between the stems, must have seen her coming; but he stayed where he was. He had been crying, but now his mouth was working down and sideways as though something sticky had lodged in the corner of his jaw; his lungs pumped in dry, jerking spasms.

'What's the matter, Mike?' said Nicky, forgetting that she wasn't supposed to know his name. But he'd forgotten too.

'The robbers have come!' he gasped. 'The robbers have come!'

Nicky stared at him, not taking it in.

'They was herding all the children together,' said Mike, 'and taking 'em off somewheres. I was abed still, with my foot, but my Mum shoved me out of the back gate and says to come to you. I been crawling across the fields, but I dursn't come no further, though you done me good once. My Mum says you done my foot good.'

'But what about Mr Barnard – the Master? Didn't he stop them?'

'They killed him! They killed him.'

Mike began to wail, and Nicky's whole being was flooded by a chill of shock at the thought of that huge life murdered. She put her arm round Mike's shoulders and waited for the sobbing to stop.

'Come with me,' she said. 'My friends will know what to do. Shall I give you a piggy-back again?'

'I'll do,' sniffled the boy. 'There's not nowhere else to go, is there?'

'That's right,' said Nicky, and helped him, half hobbling and half hopping, up the lane. His foot was still clearly very sore, and she could see from his scrattled knees that he really must have crawled most of the way.

Ajeet was standing in the lane with the basket of eggs. The boy flinched when he saw her, but came on.

'Come and help me talk to your grandmother,' said Nicky. 'Robbers have come to the village and killed the big man. They're taking all the children somewhere, Mike says – as hostages, I suppose. That means they're going to stay.'

Ajeet never looked as though anything surprised her. Now she just nodded her small head and walked up to the wych-elm where the old lady held court on fine days. The big tree stood right against the lane above the farmyard, and here in a flattened and dusty area of what had been barley-field the small children scuffled and dug, while the old lady lay on her cushions in the shade and gave orders to everything that came in sight, or gathered her grandchildren and great-grandchildren into a ring and told them long marvellous fairy-tales. One of the mothers was always there to do the donkey-work of the creche, but the old lady was its genius.

By the time Nicky had brought Mike hobbling up and

settled him in comfort in the dust, Ajeet had told the news. Nicky turned towards the tree, put her palms together under her chin and bowed. The old lady did the same on her cushions, just as if Nicky were an important person come from many miles away to visit her. The old lady rattled a sharp sentence at the children who'd gathered to listen, and they scattered.

Ajeet said 'My grandmother wants the boy to tell his story again.'

Mike was staring at the old lady with quivering lips. Nicky remembered how terrified *she'd* been when she first faced those brilliant eyes.

'He told me that robbers had come to the village,' she said. 'They'd started herding the children together and taking them somewhere. He was in bed with his bad foot, and his mother smuggled him out of the back door and told him to come to us. He said the robbers had killed the big man. Do you know any more, Mike?'

'My Mum said they was on horses, in armour,' he whispered.

Ajeet translated. Mike couldn't remember any more. He'd seen nothing himself, though he'd heard the cries from his bed, and the church bell ringing its alarm and then stopping.

The old lady spoke to Tara Deep, the mother who'd been looking after the creche. She nodded and began to walk up to the ploughmen, quick and graceful in her blue sari. The old lady spoke directly to Nicky.

'My grandmother wants to know what *you* think we should do.'

'First we've got to make ourselves as safe as we can,' said Nicky, 'and then we've got to find out more, how many of them there are, and what they're going to do next. We can't decide anything until we get more news. The only thing is, the robbers won't mind crossing the bad wires – they must have passed things just as bad to get to the village at all.'

'I just shuts my eyes and ducks under,' said Mike.

'The farmyard's almost a fort already,' said Nicky. 'We could get food and water in, and the sheep, and strengthen it. And as soon as it's dark I'll go down across the fields and try and find somebody I know. Mr Tom's house has its back to the school playground, and then there's a path and then fields, so I might be able to get to him without going through the village at all. After all, we aren't really sure that Mike's got his story right – his mother must have been very hurried and worried.'

Ajeet had been translating as Nicky went along. The old lady raised a ringed hand, palm towards Nicky in a sort of salute, and answered. Ajeet laughed.

'My grandmother says that you will make a very good wife for a soldier some day,' she said.

Nicky nodded, unsmiling. She was frightened, of course, by what she had suggested, but another part of her felt a strange, grim satisfaction in the risks and dangers. They would force her to rebuild the armour round her heart, which during the last few weeks she had allowed to become so full of chinks and weaknesses. She bowed her head and stared at the scuffled dust; at the thought of the coming action her heart began to hammer – as though there were a small smithy in there, retempering the rusted steel.

By now the men were trooping down from the field, talking excitedly and looking north-east across the swooping acres to where the church tower stood peaceful among its limes. The women called their own children to them as they came, and cajoled them into stillness and silence. A big orderly circle gathered under the wych-elm, the men stopped chattering and the old woman spoke. Nicky heard her own name jut out from the fuzz of Punjabi; heads turned towards her. Then, as usual, twenty voices broke into argument together; the old lady screeched, and Uncle Jagindar was talking alone. Voices grunted agreement. He turned to Nicky.

'This sounds dangerous,' he said, 'but we can send a guard with you.'

'I don't think it's very dangerous,' said Nicky. 'If they catch me, they'll think I'm one of the village children and put me with the others as a hostage. But I don't see why they should – they can't watch the whole village, all the way round. If you do send a guard, you won't have so many men for the defence up here, supposing they decided to attack tonight, which would be the sensible thing for them. It'd be a waste of our men. You'll need sentries all night, too.'

She could see heads nodding.

'Perhaps Gopal could come with me,' she said. 'Not to fight or anything, but to bring back news if I do get caught. The thing is, I'm sure I'm the only person Mr Tom or any of them would talk to, so it's no use any of you going. They're a bit scared of *me*, but not half so much as they are of *you*. That's right, isn't it, Mike?'

'Yes, that's right,' he whispered, staring round at the dark and bearded faces.

'And we've got to *know*, haven't we?' she said. 'We can't decide anything till then.'

Uncle Jagindar wheeled to the ring of Sikhs.

'That is agreed, my friends?' he asked.

'Agreed,' boomed the council.

He started to allot tasks in Punjabi. Gopal came, serious-faced, to Nicky.

'Our job is to eat and rest,' he said. 'Mike looks as if he needed a rest too.'

The boy nodded, but they had to help him to his feet and support him, swaying, down to the farmyard. Already the water-carriers were bringing bucket after bucket from the clanking well, while the carts creaked up from the farm

house with larderfuls of dry stores and tins. Sacks of charcoal were carried in from the smithy, for cooking, and
mounds of hay down from the big barn for the sheep. Soon
the sheep themselves flooded, baaing with amazement, into
the bustling square. The cooped hens were trundled up the
lane; barrows of blankets and bedding came from the
houses, sacks of new corn from the storage towers. The old
lady was ensconced in an open stall, and the holy book
carried reverently in from the bungalow.

As dusk fell the courtyard was still a shouting and bleat-
ing and cackling confusion. The communal supper was going to be very late, cooked on the faint-flamed and smoke-
less charcoal instead of the roaring logs they'd used when
they first spent a night there. But Nicky had already eaten;
her fair hair was covered with a dark scarf, she wore a navy-
blue jersey and a pair of dark grey trousers belonging to
Gopal; she would have liked to blacken her face, but could
imagine the effect on an already terrified Mr Tom if a dark
face hissed at him out of the night. His was obviously the
first house to try.

After the clamour and reek and dust of the courtyard, the
dewy air of nightfall would have seemed bliss to breathe if
her heart hadn't been beating so fiercely. Gopal eased his
sword in its scabbard, then frowned at the slight click. They
stole down the familiar lane side by side. Mr Kirpal Singh,
crouched by a lone bush on the bank, whispered them good
luck. (Five sentries watching for two hours each; everyone
was going to be very tired tomorrow.)

There was a copse on the right of the lane below the bad
wires. They headed south beside it, and on up the slope
under the cover of a hedge which had not been hauled out
because it marked the boundary between two farms. After
two hundred yards they turned east again, leaving the hedge

to slip like hunting stoats along the edge of a stand of barley. There was no hurry. The night was still dark grey, and
Nicky didn't want to reach the playing field until it was
fully black. So where the barley stopped, because that was
as far as the reapers had mown, they lay on their stomachs,
trying to suck the last inch of seeing out of the shortening
distances, peering and listening for dangers. A lone pheasant
clacked in a copse to their right.

'They cannot post sentries all round a village as big as
this,' whispered Gopal. 'Not unless there are hundreds of
men. In any case they do not need to defend the whole village now that they have hostages. They will guard the place
where they have set up camp, and then perhaps they will
send out patrols. That is what we must watch out for.'

Beyond the reaped stubble was a pasture field where cows
stumbled and snorted, invisible from twenty yards. Knowing what inquisitive brutes cows can be the children steered
to the right where an extra loom in the dark promised the
shelter of another hedge. But when it came it was double,
and a lane ran down the middle. Nicky shook her head –
such a path was a likely route for a patrol. They scouted
left, and the lane bent at right-angles; flitting through a gap
in the hedges, they found themselves once more at a place
where unreaped wheat ran beside stubble, and ran in what
Nicky, even after that bout of dodging, still thought was the
right direction. Then another lane to cross, and empty pasture beyond. It was too dark to see more than ten yards
now.

After a whispered talk, Gopal dropped behind and Nicky
tucked a white rag into her belt for him to follow her by,
like the scut of a rabbit. (If they were chased, she'd have to
remember to snatch it out.) Darkness made the middle of
fields seem safer than hedges; but coming in darkness to the

village, by this unfamiliar way, she might easily have missed her direction. The wind had been steady from the south west all day, surely. Just as she decided to stop and reconsider, the church clock began to clang sweetly to her left. Eight. More to her front, but further away, urgent voices yelled. In the fresh silence the tussocky grass of the pasture seemed to swish horribly loudly, however carefully she moved her feet; anyone waiting in the coming hedge would be bound to hear her – though she couldn't hear Gopal ten paces behind her. Encouraged she stole forward.

This hedge was double too, but the path down the middle was only a yard across. So she knew where she was, at least; this was the footpath that ran south between the church and the school. The nearer hedge was strengthened with the thorny wire she hated so much. As she squatted and wondered whether there'd be a gap further along, Gopal edged quietly up beside her.

'Barbed wire?' he whispered. 'Wait a moment.'

He crouched by the fence, holding some sort of tool in his hand. Two clicks, and he dragged a strand of wire away.

'My very own notion,' he whispered. 'Wire cutters. You can crawl through now. Is it far from here?'

'Only across the playing-field.'

'Then tie your rag to the other hedge so that we can find the place coming back.'

Most of the householders in the council estate kept a dog, but Mr Tom preferred his scarred old tabby; so if they came up straight behind the right house there oughtn't to be any barking. Nicky lay in the sodden grass and tried to make out the roof-lines; Mrs Bower's chimney, next door, had a big hunched cowl. So . . .

Only firelight showed through his back parlour window. Nicky edged an eye above the sill, hoping that he hadn't gone to bed yet. No. He was curled by the dying fire, his head in his hands but held so low that it was almost on his knees; he looked very old and beaten. Nicky tapped cautiously on the pane. At the third tap he looked over his shoulder like a haunted man, and then put his head back between his hands. She kept on tapping, in a steady double rhythm which couldn't have been caused by anything accidental, such as a flying beetle. At last he staggered from the chair, crossed the room and opened the window half an inch.

'Who's there?' he whispered.

'Me. The girl from the Devil's Children. I want to talk to you.'

'I'll have nothing to do with you,' he hissed, and tried to shut the window. But Nicky was ready for him and jammed the hilt of her knife into the crack.

'We want to help you,' she whispered. 'But we can't until we know what's happening.'

'How many o' you's out there, then?'

'Only me and a boy. He'll rap on the window if he hears anyone coming.'

'OK,' said Mr Tom after a pause. 'I'll let you in.'

'I'll climb through the window,' said Nicky. He opened it wide and she flicked herself through. The moment she was in he fastened it tight, while Nicky tucked herself into a corner where she couldn't be seen from outside.

'Sit like you were sitting before,' she suggested. 'Talk as though you were talking to yourself. Mike Sallow came up to the farm and told us that robbers had come to the village and killed Mr Barnard and taken all the children somewhere.'

'True enough,' groaned Mr Tom. 'They killed the Master. I was there, waiting for the fun of seeing him drive 'em off, but there was three of them on horses, wearing armour. They charged him down and skewered him through and through, so's he never got not one blow in with that sword of his. And then they cut his head off and stuck it on the pole of the Five Bells, for the wide world to see what manner of men they are. And herded all the children together, all as they could find, and took 'em down to a barn behind White House; and they put 'em in a loft with a pile of hay and timber down below, and they made old Maxie cry through the streets that they'll set fire to the whole shoot if they have a mite more trouble out of us during their stay.'

'How long will that be?' said Nicky.

'As long as there's a morsel left to eat, that's my guess. And the Master was that set on us coming through the winter short of starving that we've barnfuls of stores waiting. You mark my words, we'll have 'em for months yet.'

'How many of them are there?'

'Thirty. Maybe thirty-five.'

'But there must be more than a hundred men in the village!'

'I know what you're thinking, girl, but they fell on us that sudden, and we hadn't nothing to fight 'em with, save a few cudgels. The Master, he'd been set on getting us swords, so he could have his own little army, but your folk wouldn't make 'em for us, remember? And these robbers come with spears, and horsemen in armour, and now they've got the children – though I've none of my own, thank God – and we're bound hand and foot, hand and foot.'

'Do you think they'd actually burn the children if there was trouble?'

'I don't know, a course; but I do know they'd do *something*, and something pretty cruel, too. There was one of 'em, one of the ones on horseback, and while the footmen were hacking off the Master's head I saw him throw back his helmet and wipe his face. Curly hair, he had, and a broken nose, though he was scarce more than a boy. And when he saw Arthur's head dripping up there on the pole, he laughed like a lover. Like a lover in spring. I slunk away and come back here, and the rest I know from Maxie's crying.'

He had been half out of his chair, glaring round the room as he tried to tell her the horror of his story, but a faint rap on the window made him shrink and curl like a snail. Nicky made a dart for the window, heard the footsteps, knew it was too late and slid herself under an old Put-U-Up bed where she lay, barely breathing, against the wall. A hard fist thundered at the front door. She could see Mr Tom's feet rise from the floor, as though he were trying to curl himself even further into his chair.

'Go and answer him,' whispered Nicky. 'It'll be worse if you don't.'

The feet doddered back to the floor. The legs stumbled past the dying fire. Then a bolt was drawn, slap. Then voices.

'What's your name, Gaffer?'

'T-t-tom Pritchard.'

'Tom Pritchard, eh? Fetch us each a mug of ale, Tom Pritchard.'

More than one of them, then.

Shufflings, another door moving, palsied clinking of glass, more shufflings. Silence. Then the smash and tinkle of deliberately dropped tumblers.

'We hear you were a crony of the big man's, Tom Pritchard.'

'N-n-no, not me. He broke my fork a-purpose.'

'What do you know about the lot they call the Devil's

Children, Tom Pritchard? We hear as you had dealings with 'em.'

'N-n-not much. They live up at Booker's, t'other side of the bad wires. Three months back they came here. I had a bit of dealing with the girl as lives with them. She's an ordinary girl, to look at. The Master wouldn't have none of 'em but her in the village, and then only to do dealings in smithwork. They make and mend iron for us, they do, and sometimes I helped with the dealings. I never seen none of the others, saving the girl.'

'Ah.'

A low discussion.

'What are you doing still dressed this time o' night, Tom Pritchard? Thinking of going out, eh?'

'I . . . I couldn't sleep. I was sitting by the fire. I hadn't a light showing. I heard the orders.'

'At least you ain't deaf, then, Tom Pritchard. Well, it's time good little gaffers were in bed, even them that can't sleep. I want to see you going up them stairs, Tom Pritchard. You can sleep now, gaffer. The Devil's Children needn't fright your dreams no more, not now we're here to look after you. We'll nip up there and sort 'em out for you, soon as we're settled. Up you go now, like a good gaffer.'

A grunt, and the stumble and thud of Mr Tom being shoved so hard along the hallway that he fell. Slow steps on the stairs. More talk at the porch, then footsteps coming, but turning off through the other door. A curse as something fell from a larder shelf. Voices in the hallway.

'Nice drop of ale they brew, leastways.'

'Yeah. Cosy old spot to winter out. Scour around for more hosses, get them Devil's Children to run us up armour for the lot of us . . .'

'How'll you manage that, then?'

'Same as here. Devil's Children got children of their own, ain't they?'

Laughter.

'Be getting along then. Hey, Maxie, who's next?'

The crow of the clerk's voice from the street, shrill with terror.

'Sim Jenkins, sir.'

Heels crunching through the broken tumblers on the doorstep. Going.

Nicky lay in the stillness and counted two thousand. She had an instinct that the robbers were the sort of people who would do the thing properly, when they wanted to scare a village into obedient terror. They wouldn't leave Mr Tom quivering in the shameful dark without letting him know that they were still keeping an eye on him. And sure enough, when she was in the sixteen hundreds, another light tap came from the window. Thirty seconds later the front door slammed open, feet drummed on the stairs, more doors crashed and banged upstairs, and the hard voice shouted 'Just come to tuck you up, gaffer. See that you *are* in bed, eh? Sweet dreams.'

Feet on the stairs again, and the door walloping shut, and the crunched glass. Then the dreary business of starting once more at one, two, three ...

She was so stiff when she edged the window open that she had to clamber through like an old woman. Half way up the garden Gopal floated beside her from behind the runner beans; he touched her cheek with his hand in gentle welcome, then led the way back across the school playground to where the faint whiteness of their rag in the hedge marked the cut wires.

They took the journey home as carefully as they'd come, but nothing stopped or even scared them until their own sentry hissed at them out of his hiding and made their tired hearts bounce. Though it was well past midnight, every adult Sikh was awake and waiting in the dark farmyard. Nicky told her story in English, breaking it into short lengths so that Uncle Jagindar could turn it into Punjabi for the old lady. The pauses while he spoke enabled her to think, so that she left nothing out. When she had finished, five of the men crept out to relieve the sentries; for them she told the whole story all over again. Now every Sikh knew, and Nicky could sleep.

They held a council as soon as breakfast and the morning prayers were over. Daylight meant that Gopal and Harpit and the other children could stand sentry; from the upstairs windows of the farmhouse, from the hayrick in the big barn, from the upper branches of the wych-elm, every scrap of country could be seen. The sheep were driven out to a new pen, close to the farmyard, but the hens were left to cluck and scrattle while the council talked. Nicky was there, with Ajeet to tell her what was said. Otherwise there was nobody younger than Kewal.

'Uncle Jagindar is asking if there is anyone who thinks we must move from here ... they all say no ... Mr Kirpal Singh says we can either wait and defend ourselves before they attack us, or attack them before they are ready ... Aunt Neena says they may not attack us ... several people say they will ... my grandmother is calling for quiet ...'

'Nicky,' said Uncle Jagindar, 'you heard the men say they would not leave us alone, I think.'

'Yes,' said Nicky. 'They told Mr Tom that they were going to come and, er, "sort you out" as soon as they were settled in the village. And they want you to make more armour for them. They were going to take the children as hostages.'

The murmur of voices broke into fresh clamour. Ajeet sorted out what mattered.

'Mr Wazir Singh says we could defend ourselves here for ever. My father says no, not against thirty-five men with the only water on the other side of the road. My grandmother says the place would be a trap – a week, safe; a month, death. Mr Wazir Singh says how can fifteen men attack thirty-five. And they have hostages, my mother says. Take them at dawn before they are ready, says Uncle Jagindar. Take the barn where the children are first, says the Rissaldar. Kill as many as we can in their beds, says my grandmother. My father says first we must watch them, to find out where the sentries are and what they do, especially at night. Scouts must go and watch, says Uncle Jagindar, but they must be careful not to be seen lest they put the robbers on their guard. Watch for two nights, strike on the third, says my grandmother. Mr Surbans Singh says that meanwhile we must seem to be farming exactly as usual, but keep a secret watch out everywhere round the farm. They will send scouts up soon. Aunt Neena says that the children must stay near the farmyard. My grandmother tells me to tell you that the order includes you, Nicky ...' Nicky nodded, to show she had understood.

'... now the Rissaldar says we must pretend to be felling wood for the winter and cut the nearest trees in the row beyond the cottage so that they cannot creep up on us that way. And set fire to the barley, says my grandmother ...'

'Nicky,' said Uncle Jagindar, 'is there anything more? You know the village and we do not.'

'I think White House must be that very big one out on the far side, but I haven't seen it since we first came through. The other thing is the hostages. We've got to think of a plan to keep them safe. It's not just because they're children. If we attack the robbers and the robbers kill the children in revenge, then the village will come and massacre all of us. There're over a hundred men in Felpham, and once they really get angry ...'

'You are right,' said Uncle Chacha. 'We must be quick and careful when the time comes. And we must be ready to run away if we fail.'

The council shambled on, going over the same points several times, but slowly reaching the practical business of sentry-duty and scout-duty. At last they all dispersed to the tense charade of pretending to be innocent farmers while watching every hedge and hollow in case it should hide an ambush, and at the same time planning a murderous on-slaught on an army more than twice their size. There was one false alarm that day: the enemy spy, sneaking up the line of trees in the dusk, turned out to be Mrs Sallow be-draggled and terrified but determined to know whether her son was safe. She sat in silence by Mike's straw, but after supper Nicky wheedled out of her some useful news of the robbers' arrangements.

Next day tempers were short with lack of sleep. The men took turns to rest, but some had to be on show for the bene-fit of the robber spies who lurked along the hillside; they thought they spotted three of these, but had to act as if they hadn't.

In the dark hour after the third midnight a whisper went round the farmyard. The women turned out with swords and spears to stand sentry, while the raiding party stole up the hill; fifteen grown men, and four lads. And Nicky. If the first phase of attack succeeded, somebody would have to keep the rescued children from squealing panic, or the sleeping robbers would be woken and the second phase ruined. And that would have to be Nicky.

She thought she was the youngest of the long line creeping through the dark, until a hand took hers. It was Ajeet. None of the men noticed the extra child.

The wide loop round the village, taken at a stalker's pace, with many pauses, lasted hours, but they were still too early.

In that first faint greyness when the birds begin to whistle in the copses, they struck.

7

BLOOD ON THE SWORDS

NICKY lay on her stomach on the chill bank of a ditch; or perhaps it was the beginnings of a stream, for her legs were wet to the knee, despite the dry spell they'd been having. To left and right of her, like troops waiting to attack from a trench, was the tiny Sikh army. The blackness of night seemed no less than it had been, but now she could be sure of the hulk of the barn; the big house, over to her right, was still an undistinguishable mass of roof and treetops and out-buildings. She was rubbery cold, and thankful that the Sikhs (full of the sensible instincts of campaigning) had made her wear twice the clothes she'd thought she'd need.

In the dark ahead of her Uncle Chacha was stalking the sentry. Two of the robbers slept in the barn, taking turn and turn to watch outside while the other slept by a brazier. An oil-soaked torch was ready there, which the inside man could thrust into the brazier and bring to crackling life. Dry straw, dry hay, dry brushwood were heaped along the tarred timber of the walls; and there were two wicked cars there, whose tanks would explode if the fire blazed hot enough. The whole room was a bomb, and above it slept the children. (Mrs Sallow had told them these details, because the robbers had shown the mothers of Felpham their precautions on the very first morning.) The Sikh scouts had studied the movements of the sentries; and the first thing was to catch the outside one just before the time for the last change-over. About now, in this dimness . . .

Only the nervy ears of the watchers in the ditch could

have caught that faint thud. There was no cry. Shadows
shifted to her left – Uncle Jagindar and the Rissaldar stealing forward. Three short raps and a long pause and two
more short raps was the signal the sentries used. It had to be
given two or three times, so that the man inside had time to
wake and know where he was – sleeping in a straw-filled
barn by a brazier, with forty terrified children in the loft
above.

The raps came loud as doom through the still, chill air.
The watchers waited. Then the signal again. And . . . but it
was interrupted the third time by creaking hinges.

Now there was a cry, but faint – more of a gargling snort
than any noise a man makes when he means something.
But a meaning was there, and Nicky shuddered in the ditch :
there is only one sure way of keeping an enemy silent, the
Sikhs had insisted, and that is to kill him. The hulk of the
barn altered its shape : a big door swinging open : but no
orange glow from fire beginning to gnaw into hay and timber. The army rose from its trench and crept towards the
barn, Kewal and Gopal carrying plastic buckets filled from
the ditch. In the doorway they met Uncle Jagindar and the
Rissaldar carrying the brazier out on poles, while Uncle
Chacha walked beside them holding a piece of tarpaulin to
screen the light of it from any possible watcher in the
house. Kewal and Gopal threw the water in their buckets
across the piled hay and went back for more. The robbers
had also kept buckets of water ready by the brazier (though
they hadn't shown the Felpham women this precaution)
and one of the Uncles scattered their contents about.

Nicky felt her way up the steep stair and slid back the
bolt of the door. The door rasped horribly as she edged it in-
wards, and she looked down to see whether the noise had
worried the Sikhs; but only Gopal and Ajeet stood in the

greyness that came through the barn door. The others must already be stealing off across the unmown lawn towards the big house.

Inside the loft a child, children, began to wail. Nicky stood on the top step, gulping with rage at her own stupidity

– she should never have climbed to the loft until a child stirred. But it was too late now. She pushed the door wide and stepped in.

The loft stank. Five windows gave real light. Dawn was coming fast. Sleeping children littered the mouldy hay in attitudes horribly like those of the two dead robbers on the grass outside the barn. But three were already woken to the nightmare day, and wailing. Nicky put her finger to her lips. The wailing stopped, but the wailers shrank from her as though she'd been a poisonous spider. More of them were stirring now – older ones.

'It's quite all right,' said Nicky. 'We've come to help you.'

The words came out all strange and awkward. Nicky wasn't used to being hated and feared.

'Go away!' said a red-haired girl, about her own age.

More children were moving. A six-year-old boy sat suddenly bolt up, as though someone had pinched him; he stared at Nicky for five seconds and began to screech. Some of them were standing now, but still cowering away from her. A babble like a playground rose – this was wrong, awful, dangerous. Everything depended on keeping the children quiet until the attack on the house had started.

'Shut up!' shouted Nicky, and stamped her foot. There was a moment's silence, then the noise began to bubble up again, then it hushed. Ajeet walked past Nicky as though she wasn't there, right to the end of the stinking loft, turned, settled cross-legged on to a bale and held the whole room still with her dark, beautiful eyes. Just as the silence was beginning to crumble, she spoke.

'Be quiet, please,' she said in a clear voice. 'I am going to tell you a story. Will you all sit down please.'

Every child settled ...

'There was a tiger once which had no soul,' said Ajeet. 'All day and all night it raged through the forest, seeking a soul which it could make its own. Now, in those forests there lived a woodman, and he had two sons ...'

Her hands were moving already. The jungle grew at her fingertips, and through it the tiger stalked and roared, and the woodman's sons adventured. Nicky saw a child which had slept through the din wake slowly, sit up and start listening, as though this were how every morning of its life began. Terrified of breaking the spell, Nicky tip-toed to a window.

She could see the house clearly now: white and square, very big, with a low slate roof ending in a brim like a Chinese peasant's hat. Here a cheerful stockbroker had lived six months before; along these paths his children had larked or mooned as the mood took them; an old gardener had mown the big lawns smooth enough for croquet. And now they were all gone, and the lawns were lank, and murder crept across them. Any minute now ...

A crash of glass, and a cry, and then a wild yelling. A naked white man was running across the lawn with a Sikh after him. The naked man ran faster and disappeared among trees, and the Sikh stopped and trotted back to the house. A cracked bell began a raucous clank – the alarm signal – but stopped before it had rung a dozen times. One, two, three, four men jumped from an upstairs window and ran to the largest of the outbuildings. From another window a figure flew, tumbling as he fell; when he hit the grass he lay still, and a second later Nicky heard the crash of the big pane through which he had been thrown. In the twanging silence that followed Nicky studied the geography of the buildings and tried to plan for disaster. Suppose a sortie of robbers rushed from the house, would there be time to get the children down the stairs? The robbers had chosen the barn for their hostages because it was set nearly a hundred yards from the other buildings, and they could fire it without endangering themselves. Supposing the four men cowering in the large outbuilding – just as far away across the paddock-like turf, but more to the left – plucked up their courage for revenge ... A hoarse yell wavered across the grass, rising to a sharp scream, cut short.

Nicky looked over her shoulder to see how the children were taking these desperate noises. Should they leave now, and risk meeting a party of escaping robbers, or a returning patrol? No. Ajeet still held them enthralled: the woodman's second son was exchanging riddles with the tiger that had no soul. The tiger had already possessed the soul of the elder son, but needed a second man's soul to make up a whole tiger's soul. Nicky crossed the room and looked down the steep stair. Gopal had finished soaking the straw and was standing, watchful but relaxed, behind one doorpost. He had closed the other leaf. Nicky was on the point of going down to ask what he thought about moving the children when his stance tensed. She darted back to her window.

A man had led a huge horse from the outbuilding door. A strange figure moved beyond the animal and two other men came behind. The horse stopped. The two men went to the strange figure, bent out of sight and heaved.

The knight erupted into his saddle. He still looked strange, because his armour was so clumsy, but now he looked terrifying too—a giant toy which someone has put together from left-over bits of puppets and dolls, and then brought to gawky life. He put out his hand and a man passed him up his spear; a little crimson flag fluttered below the point. Now the man passed him a big timber axe and the knight hooked it into his belt, then turned and said something to the men. Two of them went back into the stables, but third put a trumpet to his lips and blew a long, shivering note. The knight kicked his heels against the horse's ribs and the big animal started a slow trot over the lawn, towards the barn. Nicky heard the second leaf of the door creak shut, and the bar fall into place. The third man had followed the other two into the stables.

Beyond the knight a dark figure appeared from a downstairs window and stood for a moment, round as a bubble, against the whitewashed wall. Then Uncle Chacha was trotting across the grass, unhurriedly, as though he were slightly late for an appointment. Nicky could see the knight's face now, for the gawky helmet hung back over his shoulders and clanked dully as he bounced in his saddle. His hair was tight gold curls, his cheeks smooth, his nose was a ruin – broken in some old fight and mended all lopsided; below it his handsome mouth grinned cheerfully. As he came he fitted the lance into a holder, so that it stood up like a mast behind his thigh. Now he could wield his axe, two-handed.

Nicky looked round the room for something to throw, though none of the windows was near enough over the door; she might unsettle the horse for a minute, perhaps. But there seemed to be nothing in the loft except hay and children. She craned back out of the stench into the murderous sweet air.

The knight had ranged his horse alongside the door, and already the big axe was swung up over his shoulder for a blow. His armour had gaps between the separate pieces, to allow his limbs to move freely; really it was only pieces of boiler and drainpipe held together with straps.

He looked up to Nicky's window; his green mad eyes caught and held hers, then he laughed, as Mr Tom had said, like a lover, and swung the axe. The blade crunched through the half-rotted planking and he wrenched it free and hefted it for another blow. Nicky didn't dare look to where Uncle Chacha came trotting over the sward: his best hope – his only hope – was to catch the knight unawares and thrust through one of the joints of his armour. Instead she looked towards the stable.

The three men were out of the door again, two of them

carrying another brazier and the third an armful of weapons. The carriers put the brazier down and one of them pointed at Uncle Chacha. The third man dropped the weapons, lifted the trumpet and blew, just as the axe crashed in again. One fierce note floated across the green.

The knight heard it, looked over his shoulder, saw the pointing arm, saw his attacker, and kicked the big horse round. As it turned he hooked the axe back on to his belt and lifted the lance out of its holder on the return movement. The pennon dipped. The brazier party stood still to watch the fun. The knight's boots drubbed mercilessly at the horse's ribs, so that horse and man rushed on Uncle Chacha like a landslide. Uncle Chacha glanced once over his shoulder to see whether danger threatened from behind, then waited for the charge, his curved grey blade held low in his right hand. Nicky tried to look away again, but the dread of the sight held her transfixed.

Uncle Chacha just stood and waited for the lance-point. He was a round, easy, still target. Only when the bitter tip was a second away did he begin to move, to his left, out from the path of the horse.

Nicky gulped. He had dodged too soon. The point had followed him round.

But with a single flowing twist, long after he had seemed committed to his leftward dodge, he was rolling and falling to the right, in towards the battering hooves, the way the knight could not expect him to go; and then, as the spear-point spiked uselessly past, he was still falling but rolling out, with his sword whistling up behind his back in a long, wristy slash.

The stroke did not seem to have hit anything, but by the time the knight was turning his horse for a fresh charge Uncle Chacha was on his feet and picking up something from the grass – a stick with a red rag near the end. Three foot of severed spear. He felt the point, turned for a moment to wave a cheerful hand to Nicky, threw his small round shield to one side and waited for the knight in the same pose as before – except that now the pennoned point hung parallel to the sword, his left hand grasping the cut shaft.

The three men by the stables had put the brazier down and were sharing out the weapons. One of them shouted to the knight and he called back, then came again more cautiously.

His boots drubbed and the horse bore in. The knight seemed to have an incredible advantage, fighting down at the small round man from that moving tower of muscle, and protected too by all his armour. And his axe – though he had to hold it one-handed, rather far up the shaft, as he needed his other hand for the reins – was so heavy that even held like that any blow from it would surely cleave turban and skull. The knight seemed to think so, for he was grinning as he came.

Uncle Chacha balanced to meet the charge. Nicky thought she knew what he would do. He would wait again until his enemy was almost on him, feint one way to commit the axe to a blow that side, then dodge round the other side of the horse and either pull the knight from his saddle, or wound or kill the horse so that he could fight the knight level. He would have to be quick, though : the other three men would soon be dangerously near.

But this time he didn't wait. When the horse was six feet away from him he made a long skip to his right, so that the knight had to turn the horse in to him, one handed. As the big animal came awkwardly round Uncle Chacha moved again, leaping forward with a shrill, gargling shout. The

knight's axe came up, ready for him, but the fat man leaped direct for the charging horse, sweeping the pennoned spear sideways and up in front of its nose at the very moment that the wolf-cry of his shout cut short in a snapping bark. The terrified horse, bred and trained to pull brewer's drays through orderly streets, shied sideways from the onslaught, and half-reared in a swirling spasm that gave the knight far too much to do to allow him to smite at his attacker. Uncle Chacha struck with his sword and the knight had to drop the reins and raise his iron arm to parry the whistling blade; even before the steel clanged into the drainpipe, the knight's own spearpoint was lancing up into the armpit which the raised arm had exposed.

He was still grinning as he toppled.

Uncle Chacha, bouncy as a playful cat, flicked round the plunging animal and his blade flashed through the air again. Nicky heard the thudding jar of the iron doll hitting the turf, but no cry came at all. Then the horse was careering off towards the woods and she could see how the knight lay, his feet towards her, his gold curls hidden by the bulk of his armoured shoulders, and the half-spear still sticking into him, straight up, as though it had been planted there to mark the place where he fell.

The men from the stables were only ten yards further off. Nicky yelled 'Look out!' and pointed. Without pausing to study the danger Uncle Chacha lugged the spear from the carcase and ran for the barn. To fight more than one enemy you must have your back against a wall. Nicky left the window and rushed down the stairs, barely noticing as she crossed the loft that Ajeet now had the woodman's son locked in a death-wrestle with a six-armed ogre. The children sat as still as if there'd been nothing outside the window but birdsong.

Gopal had been watching the duel through the long slit where the knight's two blows had knocked a whole plank out. Now he was lifting the bar of the door.

'Shut it behind me!' he hissed. 'He cannot fight three men!'

'Wait!' whispered Nicky. 'Then you might catch one of them from behind.'

A thud told them that Uncle Chacha had his back to the planking. Peering through the slit, Nicky saw the rush of his pursuers falter as he faced them – they had seen what had happened to the knight. They were all three terribly young, just murderous loutish boys, eighteen at the oldest. Now they quailed where the hard old warrior stood at bay, glanced uncertainly at each other and crept forward with their swords held stiff and low. They must have plundered some museum for them.

Gopal crouched where the doors joined, like a runner settling into his blocks at the start of a race. The robber at the near end passed out of her line of sight, his back towards her.

'Now!' she whispered, and threw her weight against the big leaf. Gopal stayed in his crouch until the gap was wide enough; just at that moment when steel tinkled on steel outside, he exploded through. Nicky forgot her duty and rushed after him.

The nearest man had heard, or felt, the movement of the door and had half turned, so that the point of Gopal's sword drove into the soft part of his side below the rib-cage. His face contorted; with a bubbling yell he buckled and collapsed. But the small blade had gone in so deep that his fall had wrenched the hilt out of Gopal's hand, and the boy now stood weaponless.

The middle man, who had just skipped back out of reach

of a lunge from Uncle Chacha's lance, wheeled at the cry, then rushed towards this easier victim. Gopal waited his coming hopelessly, but knowing that you have more chance if you can see your enemy than if you have your back to him. Nicky, who had checked her outward rush as the first man keeled over, scooped up a turf from the stack by the barn door and hurled it, two-handed, over Gopal's shoulder into the attacker's face. The brilliant summer had dried the turf into fine dust, barely held together by the dying roots of grass. The man staggered in his charge, blinded, and the next instant Uncle Chacha's lance had caught him full in the neck.

The third man dropped his sword and ran round the corner of the barn. No one chased him.

Without a word the children walked panting to the other side of the doors, where there were fewer corpses, and leaned against the wall. Uncle Chacha picked up his shield and joined them.

'Three more killed,' he said, 'and one run away. Not bad.'

'What happened at the house?' said Gopal.

'They are good soldiers. Many of them slept with weapons by their beds. Wazir is dead, and Manhoor, and young Harpit. We have killed perhaps half of them, but a group are defending themselves in the big bedrooms on the far side. We are hunting through the other rooms before we attack them. Perhaps we will have to burn the house round them. Look.'

A man, an Englishman, was running along the top of an eight-foot wall. He must have climbed from an upstairs window. Another figure, turbaned, dashed out of a door, planted its legs wide apart and raised its arms in an age-old pose. The arc of the Rissaldar's bow deepened; then it was straight. The man on the wall threw his arms wide between pace and pace and tumbled with a crash through a green-house roof.

'I must go back,' said Uncle Chacha.

'I expect the other horses are in that stable,' said Nicky, 'and the rest of the armour. If you turned the horses out you could set fire to the stable and burn the saddles and things as well, and then you wouldn't have to fight any more knights on horseback.'

'You are right,' said Uncle Chacha, and trotted off across the grass, still as light on his feet as if he hadn't spent all morning fighting for his life against grisly odds.

'You go too,' said Nicky. 'He'll need a hand with the brazier. I'm going to take the children home.'

'That was a good throw, Nicky,' said Gopal. 'Thank you.'

He gave her a gay salute with his bloody sword, made two practice slashes with it, and ran off after his uncle. Nicky climbed to the loft with legs like lead.

Ajeet's tiger was dead, with its skin nailed to the temple door. In the temple the woodman's sons were marrying queens.

Nicky nodded to Ajeet, who put her palms together under her chin.

'And so ends the tale of the tiger who had no soul,' she said.

The children watched her in silence.

'Thank you, miss,' said the red-headed girl.

'I'm going to take you all to your homes now,' said Nicky.

A squealing like a piggery racked the loft.

'Quiet!' she yelled, and the squealing died.

'Now listen to me,' said Nicky. 'My friends have killed half the robbers. Ajeet's father beat the worst of the men on horses and killed him too. The rest of the robbers are shut up in the house, but a few have run away. Some of them may be hiding in the woods, but it's all right – they can't hurt us if you do what I say. There's a pile of flints by the ditch over there, and I want you each to pick up two of them, or three if you've got a pocket to put the third one in. Choose stones which are the heaviest ones you can throw properly and straight. Carry one in each hand, and if you see anybody who looks like a robber, lift up your arm and be ready to throw, but don't throw it till I shout. Do you understand? Just think – thirty big stones, all held ready for throwing. One man won't attack an army like that. You're an army now. Soldiers. And you're going home.'

She led them down the ladder. Ajeet came last. By the flint-pile she marshalled them into a crocodile, with the smallest children in the middle clutching their useless but heartening pebbles. But the big boys and girls, back and front, were armed with flints that really would make an enemy hesitate. She looked for the last time towards the house. A flurry of shouts and a scream rose from the far side. A wisp of smoke came from the stable, and Gopal was leading a huge horse over the grass towards her.

'The other one vamoosed,' he said, smiling. 'But this one is too dashed friendly. Can you take him with you?'

Nicky dithered, frightened by the animal's size.

'I'm used to horses, miss,' said the red-headed girl. 'I'll mind him.'

She took the halter and Gopal started back towards the battlefield, in a careful copy of Uncle Chacha's energy-preserving trot.

'Now,' said Nicky, 'I don't want to go past the house and along the road because that might make things difficult for my friends. Who knows the best way across the fields?'

Several voices answered and all the hands pointed the

same way. She chose a dark, sensible-looking boy as her guide and set off. They crossed the big lawn, skirted a little wood, used a tarred footbridge to cross a dry ditch among bamboos, and came to a gate at the end of the garden. They wound slowly up the wheatfield beyond, tramping their path through stalks which had already dropped their seed and were now so brittle that the first gale of winter would push them over to lie and rot. A sudden rustling, as of a large animal disturbed, shook the stems to their left.

'Ready!' shouted Nicky. Thirty fists came up with rocks poised – though the pudgy arms at the centre scarcely rose above the wheat-stalks. Out of the wheat bounded a naked man, like a startled deer. He gazed wild-eyed at the children for a moment; then, amid whoops and jeers, he was scampering up the hill. Nicky called her army into line of march again. That must have been the man she first saw escaping across the lawn in the grey, chill air before sunrise. She looked to her left and was astounded to see that the sun had still not crossed the low hill-top, though the air was gold with its coming. Less than an hour ago, then, the attack had begun.

Her guide led them slantwise up to a second gate, beyond which was a pasture full of cows who stared at them in stolid boredom as they trooped across. The cries from the house were faint and few now, but a strange mutter seemed to be growing in the village. The next gate led into a lane, all arched over with hazels, which her guide wanted to turn along; but Nicky thought they were still dangerously close to the big house and insisted on pushing through the fields behind the straggle of cottages that ran down the main road to the Borough.

More pasture here, and they had to skirt round a marshy piece where the stream that flowed through the White

House gardens rose. The mutter from the village was like the roar of surf, and above it floated indistinguishable human shouts. Looking to her right as they slanted down towards the uproar, Nicky saw a slow column of smoke billowing up into the blissful morning. She realized what had happened.

'Run!' she cried. 'Run but keep together!'

'If they didn't reach the road in time, a hundred maddened villagers would be roaring down to the big house to slaughter every living thing there, Sikh or robber. It was no use reaching the road alone – she had to come with all the children, safe. The villagers had seen the smoke from the stables and decided that the robbers had fired the barn where their hostages lay. And it would be the Sikhs' fault.

The line moved down hill, slowed to the pace of exhausted and ill-fed six-year-olds stumbling through the tussocks.

'You three,' gasped Nicky to the older ones nearest her, 'run to the road. Try to stop the village attacking my friends. Tell them all the children are safe.'

The messengers went down the slope in a happy freewheeling gallop, as if it had been a game for a summer evening. Nicky grabbed the wrists of the two smallest children and half-helped, half-hauled them over the hummocky turf. Other children dropped their flints and copied her. And here was a path, a narrow channel between the wall of a chapel and the fence of a pub garden, and now they were in the road, gasping, while the three messengers shrank from the roaring tide of the enraged village as it poured down the road towards them, led by little old Maxie waving a carpenter's hammer. The men were yelling, but the women were silent, and they were more terrible still: marching in their snowy aprons, faces drawn into grey lines with rage and weeping, fingers clenched round the handles of carving-knives and cleavers.

Terrified by the sight, Nicky's army melted to the walls of the road. She stood helpless in the middle, still gripping the fat wrists of the two small children.

The tide of vengeance tried to halt, but the villagers at the back, who could not see what had happened, jostled into the ones who could. The news spread like flame through dry hay. The roaring anger changed and became a great hoarse splendour of cheering and relief. Mother after mother dropped her weapon and ran forward, arms outstretched. They came in a white whirl, like doves homing to the dovecot, and knelt in the road to hug their children.

Nicky ran to Maxie.

'Can you get the men to come and help my friends?' she cried. 'They've killed half the robbers, but they're still fighting.'

Maxie looked round at the bellowing crowd and nodded.

'Lift me up, Dave,' he crowed to the stout man beside him.

Dave and another man swung him up to their shoulders as if he'd been a child held high to watch a king come past. He raised his arms like Moses on the mount and waited for the cheering to die.

'Men o' Felpham,' he crowed. 'You know as the Devil's Children have rescued our children out of the hands of the robbers. Now they're fighting them to the death down at White House. Do we go help them?'

A mutter of doubt ran through the crowd.

'We've taken the horses,' cried Nicky. 'Look, I've brought one. And we've burnt the place where the armour was, and we've killed half the robbers. We've killed the worst of the horsemen.'

The mutter changed its note, and rose.

'Do we go help them?' crowed Maxie again. 'Or do we let it be said that the men o' Felpham stood and watched while a handful of strangers did their fighting for them?'

The mutter returned to the note that Nicky had first heard, the noise of surf in a gale.

'OK, Dave,' said Maxie, 'you can put me down.'

The women pulled their children aside to let the bellowing army pass. Nicky picked up a fallen cleaver and walked beside Maxie.

'Five of my grandchilder there,' he said. 'You go home now, girl. This is no business for a child.'

'I'm coming to make sure you don't hurt my friends,' she said.

'Shan't do that. Not now.'

'Well, I'm coming anyway.'

Maxie looked over his shoulder.

'Hey!' he crowed. 'You get off that horse, Dave Gracey, and let the girl ride. She'll be safer up there.'

The stout man slid down, grinning, and whisked Nicky up to the broad and cushiony back. She had ridden ponies on holidays, sometimes, but never a creature as tall as this, never bareback and without reins, though Dave Gracey still held the halter. She seemed a mile in the air, and clutched the coarse mane with her left hand.

But after a minute she found that she wasn't afraid of the height, because the back was so broad and the horse's movement, at this pace, so steady, that she might have been riding on a palanquin. She let go of the mane, rested the cruel cleaver across her lap, straightened her back and neck and rode like a queen.

The exultation of victory thrilled through her blood. They had nearly done it now. All through the long night stalk, and the taut waiting, and the short blind blaze of action, she had felt nothing. She had simply thought and acted as the minute demanded. Even fear (and she had been horribly afraid) came from outside, pulsed through her, and was gone. But now she thought 'We have nearly done it.' Glory washed over her like sunrise.

Now she knew why the robber knight had laughed like a lover as he clove at the tarred planks. The same glory was in him; but in him it had gone rancid.

It was a good half mile from the Borough to the White House. The village bellowed its coming all the way.

The besieged robbers must have heard them, realized that flight was the only hope now and made a desperate sortie. For as the village turned into the White House drive they met a dozen of their oppressors. Beyond, on the far side of a little bridge, came the weary Sikhs.

The village halted, faced by these armed and pitiless enemies. Another second and their courage might have oozed away as fast as it had risen; but Nicky kicked as hard as she could at the horse's sides, swung her cleaver up and shouted 'Come on!'

The great beast trundled forward and the roaring rose behind her once again. A robber lunged at her with a short lance, but she saw the stroke coming and bashed the point aside with the flat of her cleaver. Another man fell as the horse simply breasted him over. The second rank of robbers turned to run back over the bridge. But there on the other side, swords ready, waited the grim Sikhs. The robbers hesitated, and the village churned over them.

Nicky was already among her friends. Gopal was there and Uncle Chacha and Kewal and the Rissaldar, weary as death but smiling welcome amid their beards. She dropped from the horse and ran to drag Maxie out of a ring of shouting and back-slapping friends. He came without question.

'This is Mr Maxie,' she said. 'This is Mr Jagindar Singh.' The two men shook hands. Blood was still seeping from a crooked slash that ran from Uncle Jagindar's wrist to his elbow.

'I reckon we owe you a lot, sir,' said Maxie. 'More'n we can rightly pay.'

'You will pay us well if we can now be friends,' said Uncle Jagindar.

8

FIVE STONES

KAKA and Gurdial and Parsan won the fancy dress parade
at the spring festival. Kaka was the back legs of the ele-
phant, Gurdial was the front legs, and Parsan, aged two,
dressed in brilliant silks and jewels, rode in the tiny howdah
and was the princess. In fact the Sikh children, with their
unfair advantage of looking slightly fancy-dress anyway,
might have won every prize on the parade if the Vicar
hadn't been diplomatic enough to give the second prize to
Sarah Pritchard, who came as a flaunting gipsy. She was Mr
Tom's great-niece.

On the other hand the village won the tug-of-war and (to
the Rissaldar's disgust) the archery; and, of course, all the
cake making contests – there was no prize for chapattis. But
then Mr Surbans Singh won the ploughing match, cleaving a
line so straight behind his big dray-horse that you'd have
thought he had a cord to steer by. Nicky didn't win anything, though she bowled and bowled for the pig. Kewal
told her that if there'd been a disobedience prize, the dog
which she'd found limping through the January snow on
the Common would have beaten any dog the village could
put up. Kewal was wearing his gold turban and had spent all
night with his beard in curlers; every girl in the village made
eyes at him, and with his squint he had the advantage of
being able to ogle two at a time. He strutted as though he'd
won the battle against the robbers single-handed. (He had,
in fact, been very brave but not – Uncle Chacha once hinted
– very skilful, having neglected his sword-practice.)

After the fancy dress parade was over and Kaka and Gurdial and Parsan had been given their prize – a white rabbit
– the trumpet sounded for the main event of the festival.
The trumpet was the one the robbers had used for their sig-
nals: before that it must have blown in a pop group; now
it was half the village band.

The bowling for the pig stopped, and the women left off
chaffering at the stalls and began to summon their children
from their squealing chase among the elders' legs. Everybody trooped away, the younger men down to the old
cricket pavilion to collect their weapons, and the rest to line
the Borough and the short street up to the churchyard. The
old lady, Ajeet's grandmother, waited on her cart at the
widest part of the Borough and Maxie stood on a crate beside her. Maxie was Mayor now; the village hadn't fancied
being ruled by another Master, so soon after the battle they
had elected a Mayor and Councillors. Uncle Jagindar was a
Councillor.

Away to the right, from the cricket pavilion, the trumpet
blew again. This time it was playing not a call but a tune,
The British Grenadiers, which was the only march the trum-
peter could get the whole way through. A clumsy drum
rattled in support. The village stood murmuring and craning, waiting for the soldiers to pass.

First marched the two standards. Kewal carried a gold
lion embroidered on a black cloth, to symbolize the fact that
the 'Singh' means 'lion'. The village had chosen, myster-
iously, a sheep. (The Vicar had liked that, and had preached
a sermon on the text 'The lion and the lamb shall lie down
together.') The sheep was white, on a green cloth, and one
of Mrs Sallow's cousins carried it.

Next came the trumpet and the drum, and behind them
the Rissaldar and the six bowmen from the village. If you

knew the Rissaldar well you could see that beneath his proud bearing he was still sulking about losing the archery contest.

Last of all came the infantry, fifty swords strong. Uncle Jagindar had hammered and tested every sword.

There was no cavalry, because all the village ponies were too busy hauling and ploughing to be trained for warfare. The big dray horses which the robbers had brought hauled and ploughed too: neither Sikhs nor village had thought it right that three men should ride proud while the rest walked.

The soldiers saluted the old lady and Mr Maxie with their swords as they passed; they all looked as though they knew how to handle their weapons. Mr Maxie waved an affable hand, as though he were saying good-bye to a visitor from his doorstep, and the old lady put her palms together and bowed with antique grace. The procession wheeled right up towards the church, and the whole village and all the watching Sikhs crowded behind. Nicky and Ajeet and Kaka and Gurdial trundled the old lady's cart up the slope.

Mr Tom's brilliant notion had solved the puzzling question of the monument. The three dead Sikhs were of course not Christians, and neither Sikh nor villager thought it proper that their monument should be in the churchyard. But two villagers had also died, one first of all and the other by a bitter fluke meeting a robber's sword in that last rush over the bridge. These two were Christians – at least since May. So five great stones had been found, and a stonemason had been brought over from Bradley to square them up and set them in the churchyard wall ('neither in nor out', as Mr Tom had claimed). The mason had then cut a single name deep into each stone.

ARTHUR BARNARD
    WAZIR SINGH
        MANHOOR SINGH
           HARPIT SINGH
                DAVID GRACEY

Thousands of daffodils and a few hellebores and primroses stood in vases and jars along the top of the wall and in a thick mass on the ground below it.

The Vicar, very nervous and breathy with emotion, preached a short sermon from the old mounting-block beside the monument. Despite his donnish accent he managed to say what everybody felt was right, about how the two communities needed each other, both in peace and war. Uncle Jagindar read a brief prayer in Punjabi and then translated it into English, adding that words like 'courage' and 'love' meant the same thing in any language. Finally the trumpet played 'God Save the Queen', just as if anybody knew what had happened to the Queen since May. Everyone cheered.

'Very English,' whispered Kewal in Nicky's ear. She trod on his foot, on purpose.

The army dispersed and the weapons were put away, though many of the villagers now copied the Sikhs and wore their swords wherever they went; the men relaxed and chatted while the women got supper ready and the village children taught the Sikh children how a maypole worked and the bigger boys played football. Nicky noticed an odd group round the old lady's cart, Mr Maxie and Mr Tom and Neena and Uncle Jagindar, all talking earnestly. Quite often one of them would glance across to where she sat against the pavilion wall fondling her stray dog's ears.

It was a lucky night, warmer than usual for April, under a dull sky. Stars would have been pretty but would have meant frost, which no one wanted either for sitting out in or for the sake of vegetable patches which were sown and showing. But even in that comparative mildness they were glad to sit within feel of the huge bonfires which had been built at the bottom of the recreation ground. The spit-roast mutton was very good, and the home-baked bread much nicer than chapattis, Nicky decided.

After supper she didn't feel like joining in anything, though there was dancing between the bonfires – whole lines or circles of dancers moving in patterns with a prancing motion which overcame the roughness of the turf, while Mr Tom's lion-headed fiddle sawed out the six-hundred-year-old tunes. Ajeet had attracted a ring of small children round her, a little beyond the circle, and was telling them a story which made some of them tumble about with laughter. Nicky sat and leaned her back against the wheel of the old lady's cart and longed to be less stupid at Punjabi, so that she could talk to her without a translator. They were somehow the same kind of people, Nicky knew, herself and the old lady – hard, practical, wild, loving. But though Ajeet or Gopal gave her a long lesson every day, so that she could now understand quite a bit of the talk, she couldn't speak more than the easiest sentences back. She had never been any good at languages, not French, not German, and now not Punjabi.

So she leaned against the wheel and watched the pattern of dancers in the orange light of the bonfires, and the huge oval of faces, and the sudden fountain of curling sparks that erupted when a log collapsed. Neena came out of the dark and sat beside her.

'Are you happy, Nicky?'

'No, I don't think so. I don't know. I ought to be, but I'm not.'

'What do you want?'

'I don't know that either.'

'We've been talking about you.'

'Yes, I noticed.'

'We think it's time we tried to get you back to your own family.'

'Please don't talk about it. Please!'

'No, listen, Nicky. Mr Maxie's cousin is a sailor at Dover. Mr Maxie sent a message to him and he heard the answer yesterday. Ever since . . . since all these changes happened, boats have been going over to France, ferrying people away. Millions of people have gone. And the French have set up offices all along the coast, where they take everybody's name very carefully. The French are good at that sort of thing. It may take a little while, but in the end they will find your parents for you, and all this will become just like a dream, or a story that Ajeet tells.'

'But why should anyone take me to France? What can I do in exchange?'

'We will pay them.'

'But no one's got any money, not any more.'

'The smallest of my mother's rings would buy a fishing-boat ten times over. And she would give every jewel she owns to make you happy, Nicky. I sometimes think she loves you more than any of her own children or grand-children. It is strange, is it not, how sometimes a soul will speak to a soul across language, across the generations, across every difference of race and birth and breeding.'

Neena spoke some sentences of Punjabi. Nicky knew enough to understand that she was translating what she had just said. Nicky put up her hand and felt the other hand take it, felt the hard, cold knuckles and the harder rings.

'Mr Maxie's cousin will come and fetch you next week,' said Neena. 'He will see you safely right out to the middle of the Channel, where the big ships wait and the madness ends. Mrs Sallow insists that she will go with you as far as the sea, so that you are not among strangers.'

'I don't want to go,' said Nicky, 'I daren't.'

'But why? You have dared and adventured much more terrible things. This should not frighten you.'

'It's not that kind of fright. It's ... I don't want to explain.'

Neena spoke quietly in Punjabi, and there was a short silence.

'Nick-ee,' said the old voice above her head.

'Ai?' said Nicky.

The old lady began to speak, her voice dry and quiet, like the sound of a snake rustling across hot rocks in her own far country. This time it was she who spoke in short sentences, so that Neena could translate.

'Nicky, you are in danger. It is not the sort of danger we have fought through this last year. It is inside you. We have been in bad times. We have all had to be hard and fierce. But you have made yourself harder and fiercer than any of us, even than us Sikhs. In bad times you have to wear armour round your heart, but when times are better you must take it off. Or it becomes a prison for your soul. You grow to the shape of it, as a tortoise grows to the shape of its shell. Nicky, you must go to a place where you can take your armour off. That place is your parents' hearth.'

Nicky felt a chill in her bones which was not the chill of the night air. The small smithy under her ribs started its hammering and in her mind's eye she saw the iron doll topple, grinning and jointless, from his huge horse.

'How do you know about the armour?' she whispered.

Neena translated, and the old lady's cackling laugh surprised the night. Then the snake-rustling sentences began again.

'I was married when I was twelve. To a man I had never seen. It was the custom of our people. I loved my parents and my brothers and sisters and our happy house, and then I was taken away from them. I too put armour round my heart. But I was luckier than you, Nicky, for my husband – oh, how old he seemed – was kind and patient and clever. He made a place, a world, in which I wanted to take my armour off.'

'Perhaps they're dead,' said Nicky.

'Perhaps they are not. Perhaps you will not find them. Who can say? But until you have tried to find them you will make yourself stay hard and fierce. That is the danger of which I spoke. It is in your nature to become like that for ever.'

And that was true. Nicky knew that her kinship with the robber knight went deeper than the armour, deeper than the glorious wash of victory she had felt on the morning of the battle. Yes, she must go. But still she felt reluctant.

'Must I go so soon?' she said. 'Next week is . . .'

'You must go now,' said Neena decisively. 'We have not talked to the village about this, but we think that all this island is closing in on itself. Soon they will have forgotten about how to get people away; they will have forgotten about France. We must expect difficult times.'

'Then I ought to stay and help you,' said Nicky obstinately.

'No. We have learnt to be careful. We will survive and

prosper. If you ever come back, you will probably find that Jagindar is an earl. Nicky, you don't have to go. We all love you here, and we should like you to stay, out of our own selfishness. But we think you should try to go to your family.'

Nicky made up her mind, as usual, in one irrevocable rush.

'Yes,' she said. 'Yes, I will go. But perhaps one of you could come with me as far as the sea. Kewal or Uncle Cha-cha or Mr Surbans Singh.'

Neena sighed in the dark, and Nicky could hear the rustle of her sari as her shoulders made the familiar shrug.

'It would be nice, Nicky, but it would not be safe. Outside these few fields we are still the Devil's Children.'

ABOUT THE AUTHOR

Peter Dickinson was born in Livingstone, Zambia, and was educated at Eton and King's College, Cambridge. He spent his early childhood in Northern Rhodesia and South Africa, though his roots are in Gloucestershire. He comes of a political family with a long radical tradition, and, in fact, 1960 was the first Parliament since the Reform Bill in which he had no relation.

While doing research at Cambridge, Peter Dickinson was offered a job at *Punch*, where he was literary editor, and he remained there until he decided to live entirely by his writing. He started writing detective novels in his spare time, and it was while he was stuck on one of these that he started to write children's books. His first children's book, *The Weathermonger*, was published in 1968 by Gollancz, and appeared in Puffin in 1970, and it is very unusual in that he dreamed the first chapter in its entirety and wrote it down. Since then he has written several more detective stories and four children's books, *Heartsease*, *The Devil's Children*, *Emma Tupper's Diary* and *The Dancing Bear* (all in Puffins). Peter Dickinson is the only crime writer to have been awarded the Golden Dagger of the Crime Writer's Association in two successive years.

Peter Dickinson is married with four children (two girls and two boys) and divides his time between London and Hampshire. His main interest, he says, 'is writing verse. A lost art, in the way I do it. I feel like a man making wooden carriage wheels for the one customer who wants them.'

A WIZARD OF EARTHSEA

Ursula le Guin

The island of Gont, a single mountain that lifts its peak a mile above the storm-racked North-east Sea, is a land famous for wizards, and not the least famous of these was a boy called Sparrowhawk who first discovered his magic power when he defended his village against an enemy horde. Later he was taken to Roke Island, home of the famous School for Wizards, where he grew daily in knowledge and skill, till pride tempted him to try certain dangerous powers before he was equipped to deal with them, and he let loose an evil shadow-beast in his land.

Every so often a fantasy is written which stands out from the multitude in its wisdom, its originality, and its unforgettable situations : this is such a book. It won the Horn Book Prize for 1969.

For readers of eleven and over.

SPACE HOSTAGES

Nicholas Fisk

Everything was as usual that summer evening in Little Mowlesbury except for one thing – a brilliant star that appeared, came nearer and nearer, and finally, with a tearing shriek of blasting jets, landed on the cricket pitch, burning the grass to a fine grey powder. It was a secret space craft and before anyone could protest the man inside had kidnapped the first children who came flocking to see it, and lifted the ship far into the sky again. And then they discovered that he was dying and they had to find out how to work the ship. For readers of ten and over.

ISLANDS IN THE SKY

Arthur C. Clarke

Roy Malcolm had always wanted to get into space, and made up his mind that some day he would look back and watch the earth shrinking behind him. Then when he was sixteen his chance came – he won a television Aviation Quiz programme, and as his prize he went to the Inner Station five hundred miles from Earth, where spaceships were refuelled and overhauled on their way out.

Roy's adventures on the Inner Station are very exciting, more so because all the information given is scientifically correct, and they give a good idea of what life on a space station really will be like.

THE WHISPERING MOUNTAIN

Joan Aiken

A boy was hesitating one sharp autumn evening inside the gateway of the Jones Academy in the small town of Pennygaff in Wales. It was Owen Hughes, and he knew some of the other boys were going to attack him.

A few hours later he hardly cared, for he was deep in the most enormous adventure of his life. He had been kidnapped by two thieves, and with him they had stolen the legendary harp of Teirtu, which Owen had been guarding for his grandfather.

How could Owen escape from his captors? And how could he rescue the stolen harp?

For readers of ten and over.

If you have enjoyed this book and would like to know about others which we publish, why not join the Puffin Club? You will receive the club magazine, *Puffin Post*, four times a year and a smart badge and membership book. You will also be able to enter all the competitions. For details send a stamped addressed envelope to:

The Puffin Club, Dept. A
Penguin Books Limited
Bath Road
Harmondsworth
Middlesex